Eastern Oklahoma Library System

EASTERN OKLAHOMA LIBRARY SYSTEM

S0-BRM-368

PRECARIOUS SUMMER

Northern Shore Intrigue Series, Book One

LYN COTE

Eufaula Memorial Library
301 S. FIRST STREET
EUFAULA, OK 74432

Precarious Summer

Copyright © 2021 by Lyn Cote

All rights reserved.

No part of this book may be reproduced in any form or by any electronic or mechanical means, including information storage and retrieval systems, without written permission from the author, except for the use of brief quotations in a book review.

This is a work of fiction. Names, characters, places and incidents are either the product of the author's imagination or are used fictitiously, and any resemblance to actual persons, living or dead, business establishments, events or locales is entirely coincidental.

Originally published as *Dangerous Season* by Harlequin Love Inspired Suspense, 2007 (Now updated and revised)

Dedication
In memory of my unofficial aunt, Audrey Dornbush Seipold, and her daughter, Mary Seipold, who left us much too soon

Be angry and sin not. —Ephesians 4:15
Speak the truth in love. —Ephesians 4:26

Chapter 1

Driving down the two-lane highway into Winfield, Sheriff Carter Harding yawned in the bright early-morning light. Today was the first day of the Memorial Day weekend and the kickoff of the summer tourist season. Each challenging summer Winfield's population swelled at least ten times.

The town earned the majority of its income in these few very important months of warm weather. And this was his first tourist season as sheriff. Making sure that the tourists felt safe in coming to Winfield was his job.

And he had some kind of uneasy feeling he couldn't identify. That must explain why he'd awakened this morning keyed up—as if toeing the starting line at a race, yet groggy too. *Coffee, I just need coffee to wake up.*

At this thought, the now familiar attractive image of a tall, slender blonde pouring fragrant coffee into a mug came to mind. The pull to go there nearly made him step harder on the gas pedal.

But fortunately, a familiar red-and-white sign, shaped like a lighthouse, caught his eye. The unique sign marked Ollie's, the local gas station convenience store. Now it almost flagged him down like a NASCAR pit crew. *That's right. I need gas, too. And I really don't need her fancy coffee.*

"Yes, but her fancy coffee is so good," a persuasive voice whispered inside him.

Resolutely, he pulled into Ollie's and up to a gas pump. The place looked deserted. Many tourists were still sleeping in after the long Thursday-night drive or flight north. Even more would be traveling north tonight. He got out of his Winfield County Sheriff Jeep. The air smelled fresh and its chill was invigorating. He reached for the gas pump, and heard BOOM!

Jerking back, he looked around. From the rear of the store, flames leaped high. He bounded inside the convenience store, past the empty counter and toward the rear. There, he found Beau, Ollie's teenage grandson, incoherently shouting while unlocking a fire extinguisher cap. The back door stood open and he could see bright orange flames outside. Heat rolled through the door.

"Are you okay?" Carter demanded. "Anyone else here?"

"Nobody else!" Beau began advancing toward the door-way, competently spraying white foam at the flames.

"Shut that door when you can!" Carter reversed himself, ran out and around to the back. When he got there, Beau had moved outside and was spraying foam onto wooden pallets stacked around the door. The contents of the nearby dark green dumpster were ablaze, too. But the fire had nowhere else to spread in the asphalt alley. Black smoke roiled skyward.

Heat buffeted Carter. Ash and sparks danced overhead. Rather than waste time waiting for the volunteer fire company, he located the outside faucet and hose. Picking up the spray nozzle, he turned the water on full force. He sprayed the pallets and, while advancing, sprayed inside the dumpster. When he got close enough, he slammed down its blasted, twisted, and warped plastic lid. From the side, he funneled more water inside the dumpster. Within minutes, he and Beau had the fire out. The soggy, still-warm remains hissed with steam.

"Wow," Beau said, lowering the now-empty fire extinguisher. "Am I ever glad Gramps replaced the old extinguisher last week!"

"What happened?" Carter kept wetting down the smoldering remains of the charred pallets, adrenaline still pumping through his veins. "How did this start?"

"It was really weird. I just opened the back door and bang-whoosh!" Beau turned back toward the door. "I gotta call my grandpa. He's gonna be really ticked."

"Don't give him another heart attack," Carter ordered. "Tell him the fire's out. And that I'm here already investigating."

"Right!"

Cold water splashing his shoes, Carter kept the hose in his hand as he edged around the scorched area. He eyed the paint-blistered metal rear door. After twisting the hose nozzle off, he squatted down to examine something lying on the ground below the door's threshold. A very thin wire—a trip wire. Someone had strung a length of wire across the back entrance.

Carter's stomach tightened. He rose and followed the wire, picking his way through the blackened debris. With the hose nozzle, he nudged back the damaged plastic lid of the dumpster. On the inside were the remains of what looked like an incendiary pack. The flames had hidden it from view. Carter nudged the remains of the explosive, which seemed composed of soggy duct tape and the rim of an exploded quart jar.

He wrinkled his nose. He hated the acrid smell of smoke and he detected the odor of gasoline. The pallets must have been soaked with gasoline to ignite and flame up that quickly and completely.

The presence of an accelerant and a trip wire made it certain. This fire had been no accident. Carter's stomach tightened more. Someone had designed and executed a simple but very effective booby trap. Who? Why?

The name Chad Keski instantly popped into his mind. Over a year ago, Chad had been removed from his abusive father's custody and had gone to live with Shirley Johnson as her foster son. Before that, he'd been known for setting fires. But why would Chad start up again, and why at Ollie's? Carter slid out his cell phone and notified the fire chief about the fire.

Beau appeared. "Grandpa's on his way. You think Chad did this?"

Carter's empty stomach constricted another painful notch tighter. He faced Beau. If both of them had immediately suspected Chad, wouldn't most of Winfield? "I wouldn't jump to conclusions." Carter temporized. "Just because in the past Chad set fires doesn't mean he set this one. When was the last time you went out that door before the explosion?"

Beau took a moment before replying, his face screwed up with concentration. "I stocked shelves around three this morning, and I tossed some cardboard boxes out here."

Carter frowned. "That was the last time before the explosion?"

"Yeah."

"Did you smell gasoline or kerosene then?"

"Yeah, this is a gas station. I always smell gasoline."

Carter grinned at the kid's touch of snark in his tone. "Is there any bad blood between you and Chad?"

"No." Beau stuck his hands in his back jeans pockets. "I'm two years older than him. We don't have friends in common or anything. We've never even argued about anything."

"Then let's not start up any gossip. Okay?"

"Fine by me. But you know how this little burg is. I cough, and everyone knows it ten minutes later."

The kid's apt observation forced a dry chuckle from Carter, even though the truth of the statement wasn't funny. "I'll get my kit and start investigating." He dropped the hose back by the faucet and headed for his Jeep, his mind buzzing.

Where had Chad been in the early hours before dawn today? He dismissed the idea of questioning Chad or Shirley directly. Carter knew from personal experience what it felt like to be the first one everyone suspected when something went wrong. By the time he was fourteen years old, he'd been the first suspect for every misdeed in Winfield and the surrounding county. And some people in town still looked at him as not worthy of being sheriff. Maybe a person never lived down their mistakes. Carter shook this off, focusing on the present. He wouldn't reinforce Chad's questionable reputation if he could avoid it. But could he?

Who could he ask about Chad's whereabouts without stirring up rumors?

The answer came quickly. The same image from a few minutes ago of a tall, slender blonde flashed through his mind —Audra. She might know where Chad had been just before dawn this morning. He suspected she'd been up, probably leaving for work at the critical early-morning hour. Almost family to Shirley, she lived in Shirley's house along with Chad.

He reached his Jeep and dug out a crime scene kit. What could be more natural than for Carter to stop at Audra's Place for morning coffee? No one—not even her uncle—could make anything out of it other than what it appeared. Then Carter's conscience demanded to know if questioning her about Chad was his real motive. Or was he just looking for an excuse to talk to her?

But, more to the point, this year's tourist season had started with a bang. And if Chad hadn't set the fire, who had —and why?

JUST AFTER SEVEN a.m. Audra Blair stepped into the cool clear air. Anticipation and jittery nerves made it hard for her to breathe. *Can I make this work, Lord?* She placed a tray of brand-new brown china mugs on the counter inside the foyer of her newly renovated Victorian house turned café. She'd positioned the wheeled counter just inside the open front door so she could serve customers, sheltered from wind, rain, and hot sun. She gazed out through the white gingerbread and pillared front porch to the small green lawn. A glossy dark green wrought-iron fence separated her property from the busy sidewalk.

Small wrought-iron café tables and chairs dotted the wrap-around porch and front yard. Those two areas plus the foyer—where she had coffee machines, a beverage steamer, and the glass-cased counter for baked goods—comprised her alfresco café, simply named Audra's Place. Along Winfield's wharf, which was across the street from her, were eager but sweatered tourists lined up to buy tickets for the Lake Superior lighthouse and island cruises. Soon they'd begin boarding the double-decker boats for the first Apostle Islands cruises of the day. She thought she glimpsed the red hair of her cousin who was working the cruises this year. White gulls screeched overhead. And tethered to the adjoining marina, sailboats and large power crafts danced on the lapping waves.

Under her white cotton Audra's Place apron, she wore a thick Fair Isle sweater and chinos to ward off the chill. But an errant shiver of excitement zipped up her spine. Though she'd been open for a few weeks, this was the true beginning of the year's tourist season—this Friday morning launched her bid for security in earnest for her and Evie. Today she'd begin to make it or break it.

Suddenly an errant thought intruded. Would he stop in for coffee today? She gave herself a little shake and forced his image out of her mind.

The first tourists of this important day began streaming

through her open gate and up the flagstone path to form a line at her counter. They eagerly ordered her coffee and baked goods. Grinning, she rang up sale after sale. Her hopes for a busy and profitable day gleamed brighter. *Yes.*

While Audra counted out change, she watched her hard-working little daughter with her long dark braids spray disinfectant and then scrub one of the small glass-topped tables. Kindergarten was over for the year, so this was Evie's first day at the café. She had insisted on helping. So Audra had finally given in and agreed to let her wipe tables. When Evie tired of this, Audra had coloring books and crayons ready for her in the foyer. Now Audra treasured the sight of Evie's pretty face, twisted with such concentration as she worked.

Behind the counter Audra started yet another pot of coffee. Then she turned to help the final customer of the first rush and saw Carter Harding striding through her open gate. He was a raven-haired man with the imposing build of a lumberjack.

Audra expected his usual routine with her—hurry to the counter and grab a quick coffee to go. But then he did something unexpected. He paused to talk to her daughter, even squatting down on his heels to look her right in the eye. But what could he be saying to Evie?

As Audra rang up the remaining customer's sale, she saw Evie beam at Carter, nodding an enthusiastic yes to him. After touching the little girl's shoulder, the sheriff, in his brown and khaki uniform, headed toward the counter and Audra. "Coffee smells good," he said, his face a mask.

In the sudden lull, Audra glanced up into Carter's hunter-green eyes. Her hands rested on the cool glass counter. His long face, all planes and angles, had always come across to her as austere. In this small community, they couldn't help but meet each other outside of work. And Audra had admitted to herself just yesterday that whenever he appeared in the same vicinity as she, her eyes repeatedly strayed to him. He always stood straight and tall. Now, something in his eyes, their intensity perhaps, alerted her. She gazed at him, looking for clues to his thoughts. Did it have something to do with Evie? *What did you say to my daughter?*

"A large black Breakfast Blend to go." His voice was as dark and rich as the sharp-scented espresso she'd just brewed. He dug out his wallet and laid dollar bills on the counter.

"Coming right up." She turned to fill a tall cardboard cup, feeling his intense gaze on her back. Facing him again, she couldn't stop herself. "What were you and Evie discussing?" she asked.

Through the open door, the brisk wind blew the sheriff's dark bangs around, revealing a small scar over one eyebrow. "I was telling Evie," he confided, resting one elbow on the counter, "that she's a good girl to help her mother."

Audra grinned and grimaced at the same time. "I tried to tell her she was too young and she didn't need to help me out."

He made a rough sound like half a chuckle. "Bet she didn't like that."

"No, she didn't. She planted her hands on her hips like she sees Shirley do sometimes"—Audra demonstrated—"and said, 'I am too big enough to help. I'm seven now, 'member?'"

"She's a good kid." He nodded as if emphasizing his words. "And Shirley seems like a good person for a little girl to imitate. I've been teasing Tom about Shirley." His face lightened for just a moment like a single ray of sunlight slipping between lingering storm clouds.

Audra tried to fight a grin. So she wasn't the only one who'd noticed Carter's stepfather Tom's pursuit of Shirley? She was glad Carter sounded in favor of Shirley and Tom being a couple. The only problem with their romance in Audra's opinion was that by Tom getting closer to Shirley it drew Carter and Audra in closer proximity with each other. And the sheriff was coming to mind way too often as it was.

Still, something else other than the older couple's budding romance hovered in his sober eyes now. She rushed to fill up the silence that had expanded between them. "You know more about that than I do. I've been so busy getting ready for business over the past few weeks that I get home to Shirley's late. I just nibble on some leftovers before going to sleep." She capped his hot coffee and handed it to him. Would he tell her what he was holding back?

"You must get up pretty early in the morning."

Her radar tingled. Just an idle comment? No. A man like Carter didn't make idle comments. What was he fishing for? Did it have something to do with her or her daughter? But how could that be?

Carter looked pained and then leaned closer. His next words betrayed no emotion but much caution. "I want to ask you a question and I want you to keep it in confidence. Will you?"

Her sense of something being wrong heightened. She automatically lowered her voice, too. "What's this about?"

Hunching casually over the counter, he took a cautious sip of steaming coffee. "Had to investigate a fire already this morning. Back of Ollie's convenience store."

The unwelcome news tightened her nerves another notch. "I didn't hear the siren."

He shrugged.

In the continued lull between customers, she wiped the counter, thinking. She lifted her eyes to his. "If it's important, I'll keep mum. What do you want to ask me?"

Their gazes connected. "Was Chad at home when you left early to come here?"

She froze. Chad? "You think Chad might have set the fire?"

"I don't know. The main part of my job is asking questions.

I have to ask a lot of innocent questions and question a lot of innocents." He said no more, but pinned her with his intense eyes.

Suddenly breathless, she said, "I don't know if Chad was at home or not. I passed his door on my way downstairs, but it was closed."

He nodded.

Avoiding eye contact, she polished away another set of fingerprints from her glass counter. "How serious was the fire?"

"Not much damage. No one was hurt."

"I'm glad." She paused. "I don't think Chad's who you're looking for. A year ago I wouldn't have said that, but he's come a long way."

Unwillingly, her mind brought up Carter's past. If this were twenty years ago, Carter would have been in Chad's position. She met his eyes again and got the feeling that the stern man before her knew what she was thinking.

He straightened up. "That was my thought, too. But setting fires can be a compulsive behavior. Listen. I don't want to trouble Shirley or accuse Chad. At this point, it would be exactly the wrong thing to do. I don't want to trigger him into rebellion and more trouble."

Respect for this man's astute analysis rushed through Audra. She reached into the pastry case, tucked a brioche into a white sack and handed it to him.

"I just ordered coffee," he objected.

"The roll's on the house." She tried to break their eye contact, but found herself unable to look away.

He tried to hand back the bag. "No—"

She held up both hands. "A belated congratulations on your winning the special sheriff's election last month." *And a thank-you for giving my daughter some much-needed male attention.*

He leaned forward again. "Will you let me know if you find

anything out about Chad's whereabouts before dawn this morning?"

"Yes, I will." *But how would I find that out?*

A bold customer suddenly bellied up to the counter and brushed the sheriff's elbow. Carter lifted the white bag in a gesture of thanks and turned away.

She watched until he strode out her gate. The new sheriff was a hard man to ignore. And he'd asked her for her help. How would she do that? It couldn't be Chad, could it? As the customer gave her order, Audra reached for the coffeepot and got back to business.

Then the next wave of customers flowed through the gate up to her counter. Toward the rear of the bunched crowd, she thought she glimpsed...but it couldn't be. No. She wouldn't have come north to the summer house yet. Still, Audra's pulse sped up. Ignoring it, she smiled and marked down the order from the next couple at the counter.

"This is a new place, isn't it?" asked the young woman with her red hair pulled back under a baseball cap.

"Yes." Audra concentrated on concocting their frothy mocha cappuccinos.

"Will we have time to sit down before the next tour boat leaves?" the redhead asked.

Audra nodded and pointed to the excursion boat schedule she'd posted right beside her menu of coffees, teas, and baked goods. She bagged the customers' almond biscotti and stated the total they owed her. Now she was almost sure that it was Megan in line. What was she doing here now?

The man with the redhead gave Audra a generous payment. "Keep the change."

"Thank you." Audra beamed at him and then turned to the next customer, a mother with flyaway blond hair and two children.

"I'll have two orange juices and—"

The crash of shattering pottery drowned out the woman's voice. Locking the cash drawer, Audra hurried around the corner of the counter. "Excuse me. I'll be right back."

"We have a boat to catch," the woman said, reaching for Audra as if to stop her.

Audra, detouring around the woman's out-flung hand, rushed to her daughter, who stood in the middle of the flagstone path from the gate to the porch. Evie stared down at the heap of broken mugs, her expression tragic.

"Mama, I'm sorry." Evie looked near tears. "I thought I could bring you the dirty cups."

"It's all right, honey." The soothing words came out automatically even as Audra glanced around, making sure no shards had hit a customer. "Go get me the broom and dustpan from the kitchen. We'll clean this up in a jiffy. Just don't try this again. Let me bring in the trays of used mugs, okay?"

Still downcast, Evie ran toward the house.

"You should go back to your customers," a familiar voice said.

Audra gazed up into the face of her baby sister, now seventeen years old, whom she hadn't seen since last fall at the end of the season. Tall and dark-haried just like their mother, Megan looked so much more grown-up this morning. But why was she here? "I—"

"We have to make a boat!" the woman at the counter called out, her impatience rising with each word.

"I'll be right there," Audra replied, standing still. The combination of unexpectedly seeing Megan and Evie's broken crockery stirred up a riot of emotion. Why had Megan come north so early?

"Mama, here's the broom." Evie appeared, slipping between Megan and her.

"Hi, Evie," Megan said.

"Auntie Megan!" Evie exclaimed, suddenly beaming.

"We have a boat to catch!" the woman shrilled behind Audra.

Megan gave Audra a push. "Go back to your customers. I'll help your hardworking little girl clean up the mess." Megan grinned at Evie.

Audra rushed back to the counter and began apologizing to the irate customer, assuring her that the next boat didn't leave for another ten minutes. She gave each of the woman's children a free sugar cookie and the woman walked away, grumbling but mollified.

With broom and filled dustpan in hand, Megan walked up the porch steps. She paused beside Audra and said, "I'll get rid of this mess. The kitchen's in the back, right? Evie is keeping an eye on the tables."

In the midst of filling another order, Audra could only spare Megan a nod and a glance. After that, the ceaseless crush of impatient customers, each desperate for that vital first cup of coffee, fully occupied her.

And, of course, keeping up with business outranked her curiosity. Audra kept up the flow of fragrant coffee, pleasant chatter, and baked goods. Too soon, all the first morning cruises to the islands and their lighthouses would be launched and her trade would slow. Tired of wiping tables, Evie came to the foyer for a coloring break.

Megan reappeared and lifted the nearby tray of dirty cups. "I'll wash these up quick," she called over her shoulder as she walked indoors. Audra had customers to serve and her nerves were jumping. First the sheriff and now her sister. *Megan, why are you helping me? And what will Mother do when she finds out?*

━━━

ONE ONSLAUGHT OF TOURISTS and then another passed. Audra brewed dark, pungent espresso and rich coffee, adding

flavorings and frothy whipped cream to all manner of combi-
nations of the two. The scents of chocolate, almond, and
cinnamon made Audra's mouth water. But she didn't even have
time to sip the stone-cold cup of black coffee sitting behind her.
Megan kept up with clearing the tables and washing mugs and
somehow persuaded Evie that she must take her coloring
breaks. The eager little girl with her long dark braids and blue
eyes came and perched on the stool behind the counter during
each slowdown.

Finally around noon, morning cruises had departed and
the afternoon ones were all booked. The milling tourists still on
shore had dispersed to the gift shops. Happily, Audra observed
dollar bills and change bulging in her cash drawer. Soon, her
summer "help," a college student from Lithuania who'd come
to improve her English and earn U.S. dollars, would arrive and
take over making coffee and selling out the remaining baked
goods.

With a sigh, Audra walked through the midst of the
tables dotting her front yard. Evie looked up from wiping a
table.

"I'll finish that for you, Evie." Audra reached to take the
cloth from her daughter.

"I can do it."

Audra recognized her daughter's "do it myself!" tone, the
same one she'd used before she could even talk. Suddenly
aware of her fatigue, Audra collapsed into a vacant café chair.
Megan drifted over and sat down across from her. "Looks like
your new business will be a success."

Audra smiled, but her mind leaped back to her question
from before, *Why are you here?* But with Evie so close, Audra
didn't voice it.

"All done, Mama." Evie climbed onto Audra's lap and
rested back against her. Evie's long legs dangled almost to the
ground.

Wrapping her arms around her daughter, Audra squeezed her close. "Thank you, baby."

"You said you'd stop calling me that," Evie complained. "I'm not a baby anymore. I'm going to first grade this fall, 'member?"

"I haven't forgotten," Audra said, a painful hole opening in her heart.

Audra's fourteen-year-old cousin Brent sauntered inside the back gate on time. Brent had one ear pierced and a tattoo on his wrist—both which his father hated. "Hey, Evie, let's go!"

Evie jumped down and ran to her favorite cousin. "Brent!" She launched herself at him and he encircled her waist and swung her around in a full circle.

"Come on, kid, let's head over to Shirley's. See you later, Audra!"

"Bye! See you tomorrow, Auntie Megan!" Evie waved and left with Brent, who sent a curious glance toward Megan. Audra watched until her daughter disappeared. A sharp sense of separation cut through Audra.

"Well, at least one person is happy about Brent moving to Winfield," Megan said. "It's too bad it isn't Brent."

"Evie's always been special to him."

"Yeah, but it always surprises me that he loves her just as much as she loves him. Brent treats her different from everyone else in the family."

"The two of you are closer in age. That's why you don't get along." Audra rose and turned back to the foyer and Megan followed her.

"Does Shirley still clean houses?" Megan asked about the kind woman who had worked for their mother when they were both children. Shirley had become a second mother to Audra. And she'd needed her.

Was Megan engaging in small talk to avoid Audra's unspoken question? "No, she runs a boardinghouse and babysits in her home. Remember, that's where Evie and I live. And will live until I have time and money this fall to finish the upstairs here for us."

"Is her daughter around?" Megan asked.

"Yes, Ginger's working the boats this summer before she leaves for more grad work in Alaska in the fall. She's still living in the apartment over the bookstore."

"Cool. She knows everything about whales."

Audra finally confronted her sister. "Megan, I appreciate everything you've done here today, especially making sure that Evie took frequent breaks."

"It wasn't easy," Megan interrupted. "She's determined to be a part of this."

Audra couldn't help smiling with pride, but then she went back to her point. "How did you get here? Mother doesn't usually—"

"I came north with the neighbors. I'm old enough to stay at the summer house alone." Megan gave a dry chuckle. "If you ask me, Mom was happy to see me go. It's been a rough year between us."

This was unwelcome news to Audra. "You shouldn't have come here today, then." She unlocked the cash drawer and lifted out the slotted tray. She needed to deposit this at the bank right away.

"Why shouldn't I come and help? I told Mom I was going to get a summer job up here."

"You could still get in trouble with her." Audra counted out the twenties and paper-clipped them together. "You know how it is between her and me."

Megan tossed her long dark hair over her shoulder. "Evie's a sweet kid. Mom's missing a lot by keeping you and her only grandchild at arm's length."

Audra refused to respond. Was it her mother who held Audra at arm's length or Audra's own hurt over the past? Hurt left over from her mother's insistence seven years ago that Audra give her baby up for adoption?

Unwilling to go over this sore point one more time, she concentrated on counting the ten- and five-dollar bills. "I don't live in the past. Evie is my life now. My only concern is to support her and raise her to be happy and well." Audra's hand curled into a fist around the stack of fives. Carrying the responsibility for Evie and a new business all by herself sometimes gave her nightmares.

Megan folded her arms across her chest. "But Mom shouldn't have—"

"I don't think we should discuss this behind Mother's back." As she tapped the stack of dollar bills into a neater pile, Audra stretched her neck, trying to loosen the tight muscles.

Her afternoon help arrived and waved hello then disappeared into the kitchen to don an Audra's Place apron.

"Megan, I have a business to run this summer," Audra went on. "I've worked more than one job over the past five seasons and saved up the down payment for this house. I used my inheritance from Grandmother Blair for start-up money. I just don't have time for any emotional…" She decided not to spell out what her sister probably already knew and instead took a deep breath. "My plate is full right now."

"And that's why I'll be here tomorrow to help out with the morning rush and keep Evie from working too much." Megan turned and headed out the front gate.

"Megan, no," Audra called after her.

Megan didn't even look back.

Audra shoved the money into the bank deposit bag and zipped it closed. *Should I let Megan help? And what about Chad? And Carter's persuasive voice and how it makes me feel?*

IN THE REMODELED KITCHEN at the rear of her waterfront Victorian, Audra prepared her area to make another pizza. The clock read 5:37 p.m. When the phone rang, she clicked her wireless headset and recited, "Audra's Place." She took orders for carry-out pizza from four to nine every evening. "How can I help you?"

The woman at the other end ordered two large pepperoni pizzas and gave the phone number at her hotel room.

"That should be ready in thirty minutes. No, we don't deliver. Do you know where we are located?" The woman assented and Audra hung up. *Thank you, Lord. This is just about the right pace. About one order every ten minutes would be perfect.*

Behind her, Brent, her evening help, also wearing a white apron, was tossing dough for her. She spread red sauce over the pizza dough, scattered shredded mozzarella, and then began dealing pepperoni over it. She hummed along with the oldies station she had on.

"Hey." A sullen voice summoned her from the half-open Dutch door. "Tom's pizza ready?"

"Hello to you, too, Chad," Audra scolded gently. A fan on high was aimed at the upper half of the Dutch door to keep flies and mosquitoes out of the kitchen. The fan ruffled the teen's long, unkempt dark hair. Chad looked forlorn, wearing his perennial tattered pea jacket. Guilt twisted inside her. The day was almost over and she still wondered if there was an easy way to find out where Chad had been early this morning. She'd like to help clear him of suspicion.

Ignoring her, Chad mocked Brent. "Hey, Ramsdel, I like your apron."

"Get lost, jerk," Brent muttered.

"Wimp," Chad retorted.

Brent let go with a more colorful name.

"That's enough out of both of you," Audra cut in. She'd heard from not just a few sources that Brent had made enemies when he'd started school here last fall. Instead of trying to get along and make a fresh start, he'd antagonized the local kids. And he was paying for it in loneliness.

But she couldn't allow this behavior here. "You two might have gotten away with this stuff at the high school, but this is a place of business. Chad, go sit on the bench by the back gate. I'll call you when I've boxed your pizza."

Giving one last sneer at Brent, Chad slunk to the bench. Audra considered saying more to Brent, but Chad had started it this time. And she knew no self-respecting guy could let such a taunt pass by unheeded. So she quickly boxed the pizza Tom had ordered and carried it out into her small backyard to Chad, who wouldn't meet her eyes. She insisted he look up from under his too-long bangs to say thank you, but then he left without a farewell.

As she watched him go, she asked herself why she still wanted to help the sheriff. It really wasn't any of her business. Her conscience replied, *It was those green eyes of his and you know it. Don't get carried away. You've got no time for a man.*

Sad but true. Audra sighed and walked back inside. The oven timer buzzed, signaling her next batch of pizzas were ready. As she lowered the door of one of her two large commercial ovens, she heard a zap, and the door dropped in her mittened hands. "What?" She struggled to raise the suddenly deadweight door. "The door spring snapped," she fumed. "Great."

Not dire news, but it would strain her back and arms and make her less efficient. Along with Audra and Evie, Tom rented a room at Shirley's large house. So she auto-dialed home. "Shirley, is Tom there? When he's done eating the pizza I just sent, can he come over and fix the spring on my oven door or patch something together?" Audra listened while a muffled conversation took place at the other end.

"After supper, Tom's got another obligation, but he'll send someone over ASAP."

"Thanks, Shirley." Audra hung up. The phone rang and Audra took another order while she scooped three pizzas out of the oven with her wooden paddle. The hot cheese bubbled and the fragrance of garlic enveloped her.

A steady stream of customers stopped at the Dutch door and collected pizzas. Too busy to do more than smile hello as she tucked the money into the cash drawer, Audra scribbled orders, spread sauce, and used her second oven. She'd turned off the first one so it wouldn't be too hot to work on.

"Hi."

Audra looked up.

Carter appeared at her door and leaned against the lower part of it. In spite of the cool lake breeze, he wore only a black T-shirt that stretched over his powerful arms and chest.

His unexpected appearance plus his nonchalant pose threw her off-kilter. "I—I didn't...expect you..." she stammered. Pizza sauce had spattered her white apron. A navy bandana covered her head. She lifted the back of her dough-gooey hand to brush away a wisp of hair that had escaped.

Dismay swirled the pit of her stomach. Would he ask about Chad? No, of course not. Not with Brent able to overhear their every word.

He gazed at her and then lifted a toolbox. "I hear your spring has sprung."

Chapter 2

Outside the open Dutch door, Carter gazed for the second time that day at the pretty woman who'd been on his mind way too much. She was delicate and kind of...he couldn't think of the exact word he sought. Something else, something more elusive emanated from her, some quality that he didn't have a name for, something like innocence or elegance. In any event, she looked seriously out of place in a white apron, smeared and splattered with pizza sauce.

Her present expression, however, communicated unmistakable unhappiness. A totally unexpected urge to protect this single mom swept through him. He couldn't recall ever experiencing this for anyone else. In the same instant, his guard went up. This was Hal Ramsdel's niece, and he and Hal had a history. Carter couldn't let himself forget that. For her sake.

"I...I didn't want to bother you, Sheriff," Audra stammered, "I mean you've worked a full day—"

Carter replied in an easy tone, "Tom had to go to the supper club. One of their dishwashers is on the blink." Had she found out that Chad hadn't been home early this morning and didn't want to tell him? Or had she struck out and didn't want to tell him that, either?

"But you're the sheriff, not a handyman. I never—"

"Relax." He took refuge in his reason for coming. "Tom taught me how to fix stuff. Let's just hope this oven door doesn't fight me." He reached over the sill, turned the inner doorknob, and let himself in.

"Come in," she said belatedly.

As Carter passed Audra, she leaned back, giving him as much leeway as possible in the narrow work area. "Which oven?" he asked, his tone turning gruff with his own feelings of awkwardness. Did Audra believe any of the ancient gossip about him? But she hadn't acted like this earlier in the day. Was her uneasiness around him about Chad and this morning's fire? He set his toolbox on the floor between the two large commercial ovens.

"This one." She pointed to the open oven and rubbed her nose with the back of her dough-sticky hand. "I turned it off and let it cool down—"

"Good." He faced the oven and lifted the door, testing its action. If he concentrated on the chore, she might calm down. Later, when she was home, he'd try to call and ask her about Chad. He hoped she'd heard something that would put Chad beyond suspicion. But from the way she was acting, he doubted it. "This repair should be fairly straightforward."

The phone rang and Audra pushed the button on her earphone.

He listened to her recite a memorized greeting. A buzzer sounded; she turned to open the other oven as she continued taking the order. The gust of the heat from the oven hit his face as he dug through his toolbox and pulled out a long, heavy-duty wire.

She hung up and jotted notes on an order pad.

He bent one end of the stiff wire into a tight U. "Audra,

I'm going to try to use this to hook the spring and reconnect it. But first, do you have a warranty on these ovens? I don't want to do something that would invalidate it."

She gave him her attention. "No, no warranty." She began arranging dough in a pan and didn't look at him. "I bought them used."

He still sensed her agitation, but acted as if he were oblivious to it. "Okay, then." He inserted the wire into the slot on the side of the oven door.

Another local, Sylvie Patterson, appeared at the Dutch door. "Hi, Audra. I've come for my large pizza with the works."

Audra smiled. "I just took it out. How was business at the bookstore today?"

"Great. I'm happy I won't have to start staying open evenings until sometime in June, but I love the tourist season. I look forward to the people, and getting to know them. Some stop in every summer. It'll be the same for you."

"I hope so." Audra slid one pizza from the warming rack, nearly losing it off the paddle before she fit it into a cardboard box. She did better with the second pizza.

With a cheery wave, Sylvie left and Audra finished prepping a pizza for the next order. But she swirled the sauce a bit too generously and more splattered her white apron.

Carter sensed that his presence was making her fumble. *Stick to business*, he told himself.

He probed and dug with the wire deep within the side of the oven door, trying to catch a loop of the broken spring buried there. The heat from the other oven almost seared his face. The task was a frustrating one. And unfortunately, frustration had been his mood all day. He swiped sweat from his forehead and gritted his teeth and continued to poke around for the elusive spring.

"Audra." A deep voice hailed her from her Dutch door.

This was the voice Carter had grown to dread throughout his campaign for sheriff. *Not here. Not now, Lord.* Still, he couldn't stop himself from glancing over, hoping to be wrong. He wasn't. Audra's uncle was standing at the door, in the flesh. Hunching up a shoulder, Carter tried not to move more than he had to in order not to call attention to himself. Why did Hal Ramsdel have to show up now?

"Uncle Hal," Audra greeted him.

Carter kept watch from the corner of his eye.

"Looks like you're busy?" Hal leaned on the door. "Hope Brent is earning his pay."

Carter digested this. So the dark-haired kid tossing pizza dough behind him was Hal Ramsdel's son. Poor kid.

"Brent's been working nonstop. We've been making pizzas steadily since I opened at four." Audra motioned toward Carter. "Unfortunately, my oven door..."

Don't, Audra. Don't try to cast me in a good light to your uncle. It's a lost cause.

"...spring let loose. Tom, Shirley's friend, couldn't come, so he asked his stepson to come over." She sent a shy smile in Carter's direction. "I really appreciate it."

No way out. Carter stared directly into Hal Ramsdel's blazing eyes and didn't flinch.

"You," Hal accused in a low, bitter tone. "I thought you'd know—without being told—I don't want you anywhere near my niece."

"I'll be gone as soon as I fix her oven door." Carter kept his voice cool, a contrast to Hal's heated tone.

"Audra, you know this man has the morals of a snake. Why would you ask him for help?"

"I'm just fixing her oven door. I don't have designs on her." Carter's old sarcasm surfaced, leaving him disgusted with himself. The wire he was manipulating caught something. Got it. He clamped his jaw tighter as the heavy-duty spring put up an active resistance.

"With your murky past—why anyone around here voted to make you sheriff is a mystery to me," Hal ranted. "Twenty years ago, when you nearly killed that kid, you got off scot-free."

Audra glanced back and forth between them. Her expression showed her agitation. A half-finished pizza sat on the counter. "Uncle Hal, Carter's here to help me—"

"Don't bother, Audra," Carter muttered as he tugged on the spring, willing it not to slip from his grasp. "Just drop it."

Hal glared. "And you destroyed my daughter's life. Getting her started on drugs killed her. Stay away from Audra. Do you understand me?"

"Loud and clear." Just an inch or so more of patient effort and Carter would see the spring peek out of the oven slot.

"Uncle Hal, Carter hasn't done anything but help me." Audra sounded distressed. She was wringing her hands.

Couldn't Hal see how his attack on Carter upset her? Carter called the man a name under his breath and then wished he hadn't said it.

Carter burned at the injustice of what Hal had just spewed out and at the same time, remorse over his past chilled him. Coaxing the spring out into the open, he gave a grunt as he managed to hook it back into place.

Hal went on muttering under his breath. Audra stood frozen between them. Brent had stopped working and was watching, obviously enjoying the show.

"I hear there was a fire set behind Ollie's store." Hal tossed out the piece of information like a challenge. "What's so fishy about it that I hear the fire chief might be calling in someone from the state?"

"I'm almost done," Carter muttered, ignoring Hal. He reached into the toolbox for his needle-nose pliers. "Audra, I'm just going to make sure the spring is wrapped more securely in place."

"What about it, Harding?" Hal taunted him.

"I'm not discussing an ongoing investigation with you, Ramsdel." Carter gripped the pliers and twisted the end of the spring twice around its anchor. His arm muscles stretched and clenched as he twisted. He'd like to twist Ramsdel's slandering mouth and tie it into a knot. It didn't help that he had done things as a teen that he regretted.

Carter tested the door's action by opening and shutting it twice. He exhaled, trying to release his tension. "Done."

"Thank you." Relief laced Audra's voice, her gaze still shifting back and forth between Hal and him.

Hal made a sound of impatience.

"No problem." Carter packed up his pliers and snapped the metal toolbox shut. *Lord, help me get out of here before I say something I'll regret.*

"What do I owe you?" she asked.

"No charge." Carter headed for the door. Ramsdel blocked the exit.

"No, Sheriff, please," she argued, "I... Let me pay you for your time."

Carter shouldered his way through the door, forcing Ramsdel to give ground.

"I don't want my niece beholden to you." Ramsdel pulled out his wallet. He shoved a twenty-dollar bill toward Carter.

Carter ignored the bill, letting it flutter to the ground. He hurried through the small backyard to the alley. Perhaps his quick exit would save Audra further embarrassment.

"Hey!" Hal roared after him. "Don't you ignore me." The man punctuated this with an epithet that humiliated Carter doubly because Audra was an unwilling witness.

Carter swung around. "Watch your language, Ramsdel." He shoved open the wrought-iron gate and escaped into the alley. "I don't want your money, and I'll stay away from your niece."

Carter marched down the alley, seething, nearly breathing flames. Twenty years had passed, but Ramsdel would never let Carter forget his relationship with Sarah. The injustice of this rankled. But at least he'd been able to hold back the truth about her one more time. What Ramsdel didn't know about his late daughter was better left unsaid.

LATER, LEAVING BEHIND the cool, clear, starry night, Audra walked through Shirley's back door into the large brightly lit kitchen and slumped onto the nearest chair. Shirley and Tom already sat at the table. She grinned at them with effort. *Even my face is tired, Lord.* She wished she'd made some push to find out information to clear Chad.

Wearing worn jeans and a carefully pressed plaid shirt, Shirley, plump and freckled, stood and turned to the fridge. "Don't try to tell me you're not hungry. I know better. You probably haven't had a mouthful since noon." Shirley began making a sandwich on the counter.

"Your pizza was great," Tom said. "Chad and I were working late at the supper club." Tom was a head taller than Shirley, with salt-and-pepper hair and laugh lines around his mouth.

Audra grinned, too tired to talk. Soon, Shirley put an apple, a peanut butter and jelly sandwich, and a tall glass of milk in front of her. After an evening of breathing in oregano and garlic, Audra welcomed the smell of peanut butter. "Thanks, Shirley. But you do so much for me already. Taking care of Evie for free—"

"Hey. She's my unpaid assistant. Today she helped me take care of the Olson twins. And even after that, she told me she wants six kids when she grows up. I didn't ask her who she'd chosen as the dad. I don't think she's thought that far in advance." Shirley chuckled.

Audra smiled in spite of the twinge Shirley's words brought. Being away from Evie since noon had been hard on her. "He better be rich if she wants six," she said. "And he better like children." Unaccountably, the sheriff's face flashed in her mind and then Chad's face, prickling her conscience. Okay, just ask Shirley where Chad was this morning. Or ask Chad?

Shirley grabbed a dishcloth from the sink and began wiping the counter. "So I take it you sold out."

"Yes, I ran out of dough a little after eight, so I put the 'Sorry, please call earlier next time' message on the answering machine and finished up the last few pizza orders I had." Audra rested her head in her free hand and chewed. *My jaws are even tired.*

"I could have come to help you clean up," Shirley said.

Bone-weary, Audra swallowed with difficulty. Wasn't it just like Shirley to offer to help when she had already had a full day, cooking, cleaning and taking care of the twins and Evie? "You do enough already," Audra muttered.

Shirley sat back down. "Are you sure you can keep up this schedule all summer?"

"I have to." Like a sudden machine-gun blast, self-doubt riddled Audra. If she were to make the life, the secure future she wanted for Evie, she must keep up this schedule all summer. She gathered her hard-won self-confidence. "It's just four months, May through August. After that, I'll just do pizzas four evenings a week."

"Well, if business is good, what's wrong?" Shirley leaned her chin on her hand. "You've got that dumped-on expression I know too well."

Audra glanced up. Thoughts of the sheriff's suspicion of

Chad and the harsh words between him and her uncle buzzed through her mind like angry wasps. But she couldn't bring up the fight between Hal and Carter, not with Tom, Carter's step-dad, sitting there.

Audra's back ached, her feet felt numb. And her nerves vibrated as she remembered how Carter's long, lean body had filled up her kitchen. In spite of the unnerving residue of Hal's outburst, Carter's presence had lingered in that confined space long after he'd left.

She didn't want to upset Shirley, but something about Uncle Hal disturbed her. Something disquieting had started inside him about ten years ago when he'd lost his daughter Sarah to a drug overdose. Now divorced a second time and forced to start over again financially, her uncle was losing control more and more. She scrubbed her palm over her tight forehead. What if there was something wrong with him?

Shirley touched her hand. "Evie told me your sister showed up this morning and helped out at the café."

Audra tried to make light of the topic. "That's right." Yes, Megan, Brent, Hal—today had been one happy family reunion.

"Why do you think Megan showed up out of the blue to help you?" Shirley asked. "Do you think your mother had anything to do with her coming?"

"No, I don't. Megan's seventeen and contrary. Maybe this is her way to flout Mother."

Shirley frowned. "That sounds like trouble...for you."

The word trouble brought the sheriff's morning visit back to Audra yet again. She looked around. The house was quiet. Evie and Chad already must be upstairs in bed. Just ask. It could help Chad. "Carter stopped by this morning. Did you hear about the fire at Ollie's?"

Shirley and Tom looked at each other and then nodded.

"Was Chad in his room early this morning around three?"

Audra hoped, really hoped one of them would be able to give Chad an alibi.

"Why do you ask?" Tom's brows drew together. "Is Chad suspected?"

Audra lowered her voice. "Chad's got a reputation. And someone set the fire—"

"Well, I didn't!" Chad suddenly stepped into the kitchen from the hallway.

"Chad." Tom rose, reaching for the young man's arm. "Now don't—"

"I didn't set that fire!" Chad bellowed. "Why does everybody always pick on me?"

"Chad, sit down," Shirley began. "Let's talk this—"

Chad barreled past them and out the back door, slamming it behind him. Tom took off after him.

Audra buried her face in her hands. A perfect ending to a perfectly awful day.

Chapter 3

"Fire! Fire!" Shirley's shrill voice echoed in Audra's groggy mind. She jerked up in bed. Below her, feet pounded on the hardwood stairs. A smoke alarm blared. And then she smelled it through the barely open window—smoke.

"Get up! Get out!" Tom shouted. Audra heard him fling open the door leading up to Audra and Evie's attic room. "Audra! Quick! Fire!"

Shrieking silently, Audra leaped from her bed and scooped Evie out of the twin bed next to hers. Still sleep-numbed, she staggered down the narrow staircase. At the bottom, Tom snatched Evie from her arms and dragged Audra by the hand.

They raced down the remaining stairs to the front foyer and out the front door. Barefoot, Audra sprinted over the chilly, dewy grass and then onto the cool gritty cement of the street. Dawn glowed just below the horizon. Against the dreary gray background, orange and gold flames and black smoke billowed skyward behind Shirley's three-story frame house. Insistent smoke alarms, still blaring inside, crashed through her mind, stunning her. Fire. Another fire.

Dressed in worn summer pajamas and a robe, Shirley gathered Audra into her arms. "I was so frightened," she gasped. "I was afraid you wouldn't get out."

Even though her heart still raced, Audra gave Shirley a reassuring squeeze. Stepping back, she glanced around. Tom hovered right behind them. Evie clung to Tom, her head buried just above the waist of his worn pajama shirt. Neighbors in robes and slippers were streaming out of their front doors—all staring at the garish flames and black smoke pouring from the rear of Shirley's house.

"But where is Chad?" Audra's voice and question didn't seem to register with Shirley. Then Tom leaned close to her and said, "Chad's nowhere inside. I checked." Tom's expression told her to let Chad's whereabouts go. Why had she brought up the fire and Chad last night? Audra's mind accused her, *This is all your fault.*

A large older woman in a head scarf and a sweater missbuttoned over men's pajamas hurried out the front door of the house next to Shirley's. "Did you all get out? Is everyone all right?"

Shirley hugged the woman. "Oh, Florence, Florence, thank you for calling—"

Garish rotating red lights and the blaring siren announced the arrival of the local fire engine. It charged up the alley behind Shirley's house. Shirley made to go toward it, but Tom grabbed her shoulder. "No. We need to keep out of their way."

Shirley nodded and stepped back closer to him.

"I heard glass breaking," Florence said, tucking a stray lock of her long gray and black hair under her scarf. Florence was half Ojibwa and the widow of a local fishing guide. "And when I looked out to see who was breaking bottles in the alley—you know how I hate that—I saw flames zooming up to the sky"— she raised both arms—"just zooming up all around your back porch."

Audra wrapped her arms around herself. The very early

morning chill easily penetrated her thin cotton pajamas. She lifted one bare foot and rested its sole on top of the other foot. But it was shock that was turning her insides to ice. Where was Chad? She clamped her mouth shut so she wouldn't blurt the words out.

Wouldn't that question set tongues wagging? Evidently, no one had noticed yet that if he'd been at home, he'd have come out with everyone else. From last night, she recalled Chad's angry face and voice. Had she meddled and caused this? Pushed Chad to act out? *Oh, no. Please, no. Don't let this be arson.*

"I grabbed my phone and dialed 911." Florence went on with her commentary. Neighbors drew closer to hear her over the grinding sound of the fire engine's motor and the shouts of the volunteer firefighters and the hissing of water on fire. "When I didn't see any lights going on at your place, I called you."

"Thank you, Florence. Thank you," Shirley said, her voice trembling. "I didn't hear the glass break, and our kitchen smoke alarm didn't go off until I'd already answered your call. You gave us extra minutes..." Shirley faltered then and began choking back tears.

"Mama," Evie said, reaching out for Audra.

Tom relinquished Evie to Audra and then gathered Shirley under one arm. Audra prayed, *Please don't let anyone notice that Chad isn't here.*

"Where's that boy you took in?" Florence asked suddenly, looking around. "Doyle Keski's kid?"

"Chad wasn't inside," Tom said and pressed his lips closed.

"Not inside?" Florence repeated. "Where is he then? Shirley, I warned you to be careful. I know you always take in strays, but that boy's trouble. He's set fires in the past——"

"I don't think we should jump to any conclusions," Audra spoke up, hot guilt simmering in her stomach. "Not until the fire chief and sheriff look into this. Chad's been doing better since Shirley took him in."

But in a flash, she saw that she was as bad as Florence. She'd immediately accused Chad herself. Just because Chad had run away last night didn't mean he had anything to do with this fire.

Florence humphed and muttered something that sounded like "bad blood."

Its siren blaring, the sheriff's car roared up the street and lurched to a stop near the knot of people huddled together in front of Shirley's house. Its red and blue lights flashed and flickered over their houses and faces. Carter got out. "Tom!"

"I'm fine, Carter." Tom waved to his stepson. "We're all fine. Florence took quick action and we all got out safe."

"The dispatcher woke me. I came as soon as I could." Carter came closer. "Everyone's okay—Shirley, Audra, Evie, Chad?"

Audra heard the concern in his voice, concern for all of them. Had she done more harm than good with Chad? But she couldn't say that now. It would only mistakenly add to everyone's suspicion about Chad. She blocked the urge to draw closer to Carter. Was it just that in his sheriff's uniform he looked equal to any challenge? Or something more personal? Warmth went through her.

"Doyle Keski's kid isn't here where he ought to be," Florence piped up. "I hope you're not going to tell us he didn't have anything to do with this. I've heard him snap back at Shirley—"

"Mrs. LeVesque, I'll be making a thorough investigation."

"Florence, please," Shirley urged, "let's give Chad a chance. We don't know he had anything to do with this. Please."

CARTER STUDIED THE predawn gray sky, illuminated by the lights of the fire engine and his Jeep. The flames leaping above the roof in the rear blinked out, though dark smoke still billowed and rolled high. Adrenaline pumped through him, just as it had yesterday morning. Two fires in a row and on Memorial Day weekend of all times.

"Looks like they're getting this under control fast. Maybe there won't be too much damage," Tom said.

Carter hoped so. In the low light, his eyes sought out Audra's ivory face. When he met her eyes they were anxious again.

Audra gave him a strained smile.

He wished he could reassure her that he could handle this, that she shouldn't be concerned. But too many eyes watched them.

"This is the second fire in two days," Florence announced, undeterred by his cautions. "What's going on, Sheriff? We can't have stuff like this happening right at the start of tourist season."

Florence's reaction was exactly what he'd dreaded. Doubt clawed him. Maybe Chad, the most likely suspect, was the fire-setter. But he'd still need evidence. "I'm investigating the first fire, and I'll thoroughly investigate this one." He hoped these official words would carry weight with Florence LeVesque, but he doubted it.

"Well, I told you. You don't have far to look for a suspect." Florence's words dripped with vinegar.

"There was no evidence to link the fire in back of Ollie's to Chad." Carter gave Florence a stern look, but he stopped himself from glancing around once more looking for the boy.

Audra stepped forward with a welcome interruption. "It looks like they've put it out."

Carter sent her a glance of thanks.

The fire chief strode around the side of the house and

approached the sheriff. "A few of the guys are checking to make sure it's completely out. But it looks like Shirley will only have to replace her back porch. We got here in time and it didn't spread inside the house proper. Shirley, it's good you had a steel door between the back porch and the kitchen and that it was shut tight. You'll be replacing it, but it kept the fire out."

"Thank you," Shirley breathed.

Then Carter saw Audra sag. He reached out and gripped her arms. "Okay?"

"It's just the relief," she murmured and pulled away.

But not before Carter felt a shiver go through her. He hoped it was due to the early-morning chill, not anything he'd done. With his question yesterday morning he'd inadvertently drawn her into his investigation.

"Good work, Florence." The fire chief nodded to the older woman. "I hear you're the one who called in this fire."

"I heard glass breaking," Florence said with a nod. "My eyes aren't worth much anymore, but I can still hear as good as ever."

"Glad to hear it," Carter said, wishing he were as confident as he was trying to sound. He motioned for the fire chief to accompany him to view the remains of the fire. The crowd moved forward with them—except for Audra with her little girl in her arms.

Carter stopped everyone with a raised hand. "Since this looks like it might be a suspicious fire, I need everyone to stay away from the scene until my deputies and I are finished investigating." He turned slowly and looked directly into each person's face.

"Can I..." Shirley asked with the lift of a hand, "see how...bad it is?"

Carter replied, "You can look at it from the alley. But you won't be able to enter the fire areas until our investigation is complete. The rest of you can go on home. It's a little chilly to be standing around in robes and slippers, isn't it?"

"Sheriff, may I go inside?" Audra asked, sounding timid. "I need to get dressed and leave for work soon."

Carter turned to the fire chief who replied, "Sure. Just don't come near the back entrance."

"No problem." With Evie in hand, Audra walked past Carter toward Shirley's sidewalk.

Carter reached out and patted Evie's shoulder as Audra passed by him. He wished he could show some concern for Audra, but there were still too many witnesses and too many gossips hovering nearby.

"Sheriff," Evie called as Audra shepherded her toward the house, "don't let anybody burn Nana Shirley's house down!"

"I won't, Evie." Carter watched Audra disappear into Shirley's house and then he led the fire chief, Tom, and Shirley toward the alley to view the fire scene. Where was Chad Keski? Carter still hoped that Chad's absence could be easily explained. But he doubted it. And Audra's troubled eyes would haunt him the rest of the day.

⊏▭⊐

AROUND EIGHT O'CLOCK that morning behind his desk, Carter folded his hand around the warm mug of office-brewed coffee, remembering wistfully the good brew and brioche from Audra yesterday morning. No such comfort today. He, Tom, and Chad sat in Carter's small office. His door was closed. It was 8:37 a.m. on Saturday morning, and Carter was trying to think how to finesse the information he wanted from Chad.

Across from Carter, the fourteen-year-old sat with an odd combination of body language. Above the waist, with his chin down and his arms folded in a tight bundle, he was protecting himself. But below the waist, his legs were sprawled apart in an attitude of disdain. Tom sat beside him, looking concerned, almost bleak. He'd brought Chad in just a few minutes ago.

A heavy feeling of inevitability had settled over Carter and was seeping deeper inside him. He spoke toward the computer that would record a video of this interview, giving the time, date, and full names of those present. "Okay, Chad, do you understand that I am recording our interview?"

The kid shrugged.

"Please answer audibly," Carter said in his no-emotion investigator's voice.

"Yeah, I know you're recording this," Chad said in a mocking tone. "Like I care."

"Cooperate, Chad," Tom urged quietly. "Please."

Carter ignored the kid's sarcasm. "Okay, let me get this straight. When Tom opened his repair shop this morning where you work, he found you sleeping in a customer's car inside the shop?"

"Yeah."

Though Tom's garage was only a block away from Shirley's, Carter didn't ask Chad why the fire siren hadn't awakened him. Kids and teens could deep-sleep through such things. "And you ran away from Shirley's last night after you eavesdropped on a conversation between Audra—"

"Why didn't you just bring me in for questioning yesterday?" Chad interrupted. "Why talk to Audra about me?"

"I was trying to keep from casting suspicion on you," Carter answered with honesty, hoping that would alter Chad's bad attitude.

"Yeah, right," Chad sneered. "If there's a fire, everybody in town will peg me for it. You think you can change that? You can't. I can't. I'm not even going to try."

In Chad's belligerent voice, Carter heard the echo of his own younger voice. How many conversations like this had he had with now-retired Amos Todd, who'd been sheriff when

Carter had been Chad's age? *I'm just trying to help you, kid. Help me out here.*

Carter took a deep breath. "That's exactly why I asked Audra where you were, Chad, when the fire at Ollie's was set. Neither of us wanted people jumping to a wrong conclusion."

Carter let this sink in or at least hoped it did, and then went on. "Now, do you have an alibi for your whereabouts yesterday very early in the morning and today near the same hour?"

"No. Do you?"

Carter pursed his lips and held on to his temper. Chad himself was a box of tinder ready to go up in flames. Carter didn't want to strike the match. "Tom, do you keep gasoline in your repair garage?"

"Some. I need it for the lawn mower I keep to do Shirley's yard and for my boat's Evinrude. Why?"

Carter didn't want to give out the pitiful bits of cursory evidence he'd gathered at the second fire. But the smell of gasoline at today's scene had been unmistakable.

There was a sudden commotion outside Carter's office. His deputy on duty, Trish Franklin, raised her voice. "You can't go in there!"

The door burst open. Doyle Keski stormed in. "You got my kid in here! I gotta right to come in!" An older, scruffier version of Chad shook off Trish's hand and glared at Carter. "What're you charging my kid with?"

Carter kept an eye on Doyle and Chad. Chad's demeanor had changed. He'd pulled in completely and glanced around as if gauging whether he could escape or not. The urge to confront Keski about this evidence of abuse surged through Carter like the storms of November. "Mr. Keski," Carter said evenly, "I've not charged your son with anything."

"Then what the heck have you got him here for?" Doyle demanded. The stale odors of too many cigarettes and too little soap filled the room.

"I'm merely establishing his whereabouts at the crucial times. It's too soon to link anyone to the fire. The investigation of the crime scene isn't complete." Carter turned to Chad. "So Chad, you were telling me your whereabouts for the last two nights—sunset to dawn."

As if hunted, Chad looked out from under too-long bangs. "Thursday night, I was just sleeping in my room and then last night at Tom's garage. I was just sleeping, man."

Carter heard Chad's sudden turnaround. Chad didn't want to give his father—guilty of neglect and physical abuse— anything to get involved in. Chad didn't like the sheriff, but he feared his father. And hated him. And loved him. A large rock pressed down on Carter's lungs. How he remembered aching with the same emotions.

Carter reached over, ready to end the video taping. "I think that takes care of matters then, Chad. Thanks for your cooperation. Tom, thank you for bringing Chad over so we could clear this up." He ended the video.

Chad's eyes opened wide. He hadn't expected Carter to be an ally. And maybe that would be good for him—give the kid something to think about. Carter could only hope. He stood and shook hands with Tom and Chad. He looked pointedly at Doyle, who blocked the exit. "Is there anything else, Mr. Keski?"

Robbed of a chance to show his disdain for the law and how much he "cared" for his son, Doyle stomped out.

Carter watched him go and wondered if Doyle had another reason for coming. Did he want to know what was going on because he had something to hide?

Doyle had a grudge against Shirley and Tom. Shirley because she'd taken Chad as a foster child. Tom because he had reported witnessing Doyle abuse Chad and had hired Chad to work at his repair shop. Doyle probably missed having Chad to kick around. Had Doyle, not Chad, set fire to Shirley's back steps? But why would he set fire to Ollie's dumpster? Carter would look into that.

———

ANOTHER DAY, ANOTHER dollar. In spite of its early chill, Saturday morning was proving to be balmy, perfect for the tourists. Standing behind the counter at her café, Audra blinked her sleepy eyes and then widened them while trying not to yawn. The early-morning fire had robbed her of over an hour of sleep—an hour of sleep she'd been in dire need of. Plus the sense of causing more harm than good nagged her, lowering her spirits as well.

It was all about Chad, the fires, and the sheriff. Sometime today she'd have to face Carter and confess that her ill-timed question might have triggered Chad to set fire to Shirley's porch. This morning Florence had voiced suspicions about Chad, just exactly what the sheriff had wanted to avoid by discreetly asking Audra about Chad's whereabouts. Would the sheriff have any idea how to undo any mischief she'd done last night when Chad had been eavesdropping?

She heard voices coming near and footsteps on the flag-stone path. She looked up and smiled, ready for business. "Good morning." She greeted four guys, obviously fresh out of college for the summer. Squinting into the daylight glinting from Lake Superior on the horizon, she drew in a deep breath of cool morning air to keep her eyes open.

Her sister sauntered in through the front gate. Megan appeared carefree and unfazed by life. Envious, Audra couldn't even remember how that felt. Perched on a stool by the gate, Evie had been waiting for her aunt. Megan greeted Evie with a big hug and Evie's responding smile blazed with a five-hundred-watt intensity. Again, Audra appreciated Megan's help and the attention she lavished on Evie.

"Wow, this place smells good," one of the college guys said. "How about a tall black coffee and three of those things?" He pointed to the glass case in front of her, filled with golden brioche, raspberry Danish, and dark sweet croissants.

"The chocolate-frosted, sour cream croissants?" She smiled.

"Yeah, maybe I should get four." He grinned.

She chuckled. "If you don't eat them all at once, they'd make a great midmorning snack." She grinned as she mentally calculated the rising bill.

With a wave, Megan walked around the counter behind Audra and headed toward the kitchen. When she came back, she was tying her apron strings behind her back. "Morning," she said, pausing beside Audra.

"Same to you," Audra said, handing the guy his bag and taking his payment. She smiled and he walked away.

"Aren't you going to tell me I shouldn't have come?" Megan taunted with a mischievous grin.

Audra just shook her head.

"I called Mom last night and told her I had a job here," Megan said.

"What did she say?" Would their mother think that Audra was trying to make Megan take sides in their cool, silent, and painful standoff?

"Nothing." As if guessing what Audra was thinking, Megan chuckled and walked around the counter out into the sunlight to start working.

A young couple stepped up to Audra's counter. They ordered lattes, fresh-squeezed orange juice, and brioches and paid a wonderful total of dollars for their continental breakfast. As Audra ran the couple's credit card through the machine, Brent slouched in through the front gate. Why was he here so early? Audra nodded at Brent as she gave the customer their receipt to sign.

Brent edged around the counter. "Hi, Audra."

"Hi, Brent." Audra thanked the customer and gave him his copy of the receipt. "You're here early."

Brent leaned close. "Dad was really steamed at you last night." Her cousin sounded pleased. "I enjoyed my dad being mad at someone else for a change. Thanks."

At that moment, Chad walked through her gate.

Audra cringed. Another scene in front of customers —please no.

Brent and Chad spotted each other almost simultaneously. Chad's walk turned into a swagger. "Hey, jerk," he greeted Brent at the counter.

"Hey, dipwad," Brent responded.

"That's enough out of both of you," Audra snapped.

Ignoring her reprimand, Brent smirked. "Someone called my dad to say you already been to the sheriff's office this morning for setting fire to your foster mother's house."

Chad lunged for Brent.

Audra leaned over the counter and with the long-handled metal spoon she used to stir some of the taller frothy drinks tapped both of them sharply on the head. "This is a place of business," she growled. "Chad, are you here for something besides trouble?" She tossed the spoon onto the tray of mugs waiting to be washed.

Chad rubbed the top of his head. "Tom wants two mocha lattes to go." He dragged out dollar bills and put it on the counter. "Don't do that to me again."

"Don't start fights at my café and you'll be safe from me," Audra said, a little surprised at herself for her actions. But they were acting like children, so she'd treated them that way. She didn't say that, however; it would amount to pouring gasoline on a fire.

"Brent," she demanded as she started the mocha lattes, "do you want something besides irritating me?"

Snubbing her and Chad, Brent wandered over to Evie and began talking to her.

Audra leaned over and murmured to Chad, "I'm sorry about last night. I didn't—"

"Cool it," Chad cut her off. "I'm cool. You're cool. The sheriff made it right."

Puzzled, Audra finished Tom's order in record time and sent Chad on his way. What had the sheriff made right?

She glanced up and froze in place when she saw Gordon Hamilton and a pretty blonde strolling in through her gate. They were heading straight for her. For a nanosecond, Audra considered running away and hiding. Why did Gordon of all people have to come here today?

"We'll have two coffees and two croissants," he said in a cool impersonal voice, already reaching for his wallet.

She hadn't seen Gordon this close up...for years. Audra's hand trembled as she reached for two mugs. Still as dark-haired and devastatingly handsome as she remembered, he hardly acted as if she qualified as human. She might as well be part of the coffeemaker. She shouldn't haven't expected more from him. She lowered her eyes. If he could ignore her, she could ignore him.

"Hey, Gordon," Brent called, walking up the porch steps.

Audra's hands turned clammy. Did Brent know who Gordon was, had been to her? Would he say something and cause a scene?

Gordon turned. "Hey, Brent. Come over and say hello to the new Mrs. Gordon Hamilton."

Keeping her head down, Audra finished pouring the coffees. Now she knew how the phrase "being steamed" came about. She was steamed right now. So Gordon hadn't come here just to buy breakfast. He'd come to flaunt his new bride. Or was she just being self-absorbed? Maybe he didn't think of her anymore at all.

Out in the yard, Evie and Megan were clearing a table together. Did Megan recognize Gordon? Audra's skittish heart skipped a beat. She couldn't stop her face from blazing. She preferred being ignored. But she knew she was lying to herself. She deserved this man's respect and at the very least common courtesy. But obviously she was expecting too much.

Brent shook hands with Gordon's coolly stylish bride while Gordon introduced him to her.

"Darling, this is Brent Ramsdel. He grew up almost next door to us in Kenilworth. He and his dad just moved up here last fall full-time. Right, Brent?"

Audra didn't hear Brent's reply, because of the buzzing in her ears. Gordon handed Audra his card to pay. Careful not to touch his fingers, she completed the transaction. He turned away without once making eye contact with her. She tried to slow her nervous heart.

Fortunately, a line of customers appeared then, all clamoring for her attention. How much nerve did it take for Gordon to act as if he and Audra had never met?

Gordon and his bride sat down. Evie walked past him and the situation twisted and cut and entangled Audra like brand-new barbed wire. Did Gordon even have a clue who had just passed him? How could a man have a heart clamped so tight?

LATER THAT MORNING, Carter pulled up in the alley behind Shirley's house and got out. *Lord, help me find some clues. Please.* He'd just finished assuring Ollie that he'd asked for help from the state in investigating both the fire at his place and now here. Ollie had taken the fire in stride and was just glad that all that had to be replaced was the dumpster. Primarily he'd been grateful that the sheriff had been there to help his grandson. Carter had felt better after talking to Ollie. But here he was now at the scene of a second fire. The back of the three-story white frame house was scorched, and only a pile of soggy blackened wood was left of the back steps and porch. He wrinkled his nose against the same acrid stench he'd encountered at Ollie's the morning before.

Deputy Trish Franklin, wearing latex gloves and a flimsy white overall over her clothes, was there painstakingly working through the taped-off blackened crime scene. She straightened and turned toward him. "Sheriff, come here. I want you to see this." She motioned him over to the place where she'd been probing the detritus with a stick, nudging apart ash and debris. "See?" After he reached her side, she pointed down to a handful of coins, which looked like blackened pennies.

He squatted down to give them a closer look, then glanced up questioningly.

"If you go back over my report from the first crime scene, you'll note that I found a handful of pennies at the first fire. I mean, I didn't think anything of them, either, just marked them down. I thought someone just lost them behind the convenience store. But twice?"

He stared down at the pennies. He remembered seeing the pennies yesterday. Pennies? Pennies? A coincidence? Or a clue?

Chapter 4

Sunday morning dawned bright and clear, the third great tourist morning in a row. It was too bad that Carter's grim mood didn't match the good weather. He paused to take off his sheriff's hat on the top step of the Winfield Community Church. Two days into this year's tourist season and he already had two suspicious fires. Would he be lucky, he thought sarcastically, and get a third today?

Pressure tightened his jaw. Through the open church doors, the old organ played a welcoming prelude, beckoning him. He needed some of God's peace this morning.

Behind him came the sound of rapid footsteps and breathless voices. Audra and Evie, hand in hand, were running around the corner and up the steps to the white clapboard church. From above, the church bell pealed the call for the early seven o'clock summer service. The pair of latecomers reached the top step and came even with him. He knew he should proceed inside and slip into his usual back pew, but the sight of them held him in place.

Evie wore a white summer dress. Audra had elegantly

clipped her own long blond hair up and wore khaki slacks and a blue T-shirt with lace at the neck. She looked good.

Evie squealed, "Hi, Sheriff!"

Caught red-handed gawking, he nodded his head politely and moved away. "Good morning, Evie."

Evie grabbed his hand and tugged it. "Sit with us."

Carter's eyes swung to Audra's. There he saw the same reluctance he knew must show in his. "I'll see you afterward, Evie." He tried to gently slide his hand from her grip.

The little girl clung tighter. "Please," she begged. "Please. I'll be good."

The pastor's welcoming words floated out to Carter in the clear air. Evie was making him feel like a monster. But surely her mother didn't want them to sit as a threesome. What should he do?

Audra touched her daughter's arm. "Come on, honey. We have to get inside."

"Please, Mama. Please, Sheriff," Evie begged, still clinging to him. He sent a silent plea to Audra for what to do. She looked past Evie into the church and his gaze trailed hers. He saw what she evidently did. A few people were looking back at them with obvious curiosity on their faces. The organist began playing the opening hymn.

"Please," Evie wheedled, her heart in her voice.

Carter watched Audra's resistance dissolve as her face relaxed and then she nodded. Evie beamed and held up both her arms. Carter reached down, swung the little girl in the white summer dress into his arms.

Audra leaned close and whispered, "I need to talk to you. Afterward."

Frowning over what this could mean, he followed Audra to the first empty pew.

Carter put Evie down and lifted a red cloth-bound hymnal from the holder. Standing on top of the worn maple pew beside him, Evie claimed the heavy red hymnbook from his hand and held it unsteadily between the sheriff and her mom. Carter glanced at Audra in commiseration. Their sitting together would not be overlooked or taken lightly. How could they avoid people getting the wrong idea?

Then, glancing at the stained glass window depicting Jesus blessing the children, Carter turned it around. Wasn't Evie more important than what people said? Maybe it had been wrong of him to show this little girl attention whenever he stopped in at Shirley's and allow her attachment to him to grow. But he hadn't had the heart to deny her. She was a sweet little kid and craved his and Tom's attention so much.

Audra moved closer to Evie and to him. She glanced up at him and shrugged. Was she saying what he was thinking—that they would just ignore what other people thought? Brave woman. Gossip was Winfield's most popular hobby. The heavy hymnbook wobbled in Evie's hands so Carter claimed his half of the book. Audra gripped the other. Evie glowed and sang loudly and a bit off-key, "Holy, holy, holy..." He glanced at Audra.

The hymn ended. Carter returned the hymnbook to its place in the holder and Evie sat down between them. A glance at Audra made him wonder if she had something she wanted to tell him.

Throughout the service, Carter fought two very different distractions. First was the dread that another fire would take place today. As yet, despite Deputy Franklin's discovery of the pennies, he didn't know conclusively whether the two fires were related. What possible connection could there be between the two victims, Ollie and Shirley? And to make things more difficult, each fire had been set up and ignited in a different way.

From outside the open window, the loud voices of a family of tourists discussing breakfast intruded. Carter picked up the church bulletin from the pew. He tried to listen to the scripture reading, but his thoughts wouldn't let go. There was nothing to connect the two fires except for the fact that they took place in or near Winfield and some pennies were left behind. The pennies might be a clue or they might not be. He couldn't take a stack of pennies as evidence, could he? He had nothing to investigate, nothing to follow up on. No way to prevent a third fire. He crumpled the church bulletin before he realized what he was doing.

Evie tugged the bulletin out of his grasp and flattened it on the hymnal, drawing his attention back to distraction number two, which was the pretty woman sitting just on the other side of Evie. Did Audra want to speak to him because she had more information about Chad or the fire at Shirley's? He sneaked another sideways glance at her. She was sitting with her hands folded on her lap. For a moment, his gaze lingered on the delicate curve of her dainty wrists and her long slender fingers. He liked that she didn't wear nail polish. He ran his gaze up her elegant neck to her determined chin.

Beside him, Evie scribbled on the church bulletin, completely innocent of the significance others might put to the three of them sitting together. She silently showed him her drawings. Smiling, he reached over to point with approval to one of her more interesting scribbles. At the same moment, Audra reached over to smooth back her daughter's long dark hair. Their fingers brushed. As if touching a hot stove, both jerked their hands back.

Heat suffused Carter's neck. He forced his eyes forward though the temptation to glance at her pestered him. The pastor at last ended the sermon with a final prayer. The organ pounded the opening chords of the postlude. Everyone stood and headed toward the door.

Other people of the small congregation greeted them as usual but with assessing looks; however, no one could afford to linger. The early service accommodated those who worked on

Sunday mornings in the summer. Florence LeVesque, Shirley's neighbor, was the most obvious about assessing their three-some. On her way down the church steps, the older woman with her bronzed, lined face kept glancing back at them so intently that Carter hoped she wouldn't miss one of the steps.

Hoping he projected complete indifference, Carter escorted Evie down the steps. "I have to get to work," he told her at the bottom.

"You could come to my mama's café and drink coffee," Evie invited, swaying back and forth, making her cotton skirt flare.

Audra replied with an undercurrent in her voice, "Yes, come with us and I'll give you a cup of coffee."

He sized up her words against her expression. She did want to talk to him, but she looked troubled. Guilt over involving her with Chad rose into his throat. But this might be about something else. He walked along beside Audra while Evie skipped ahead of them, reciting a children's rhyme and avoiding cracks in the sidewalk.

In an undertone, Audra explained, "I feel so guilty about Chad. Did Tom tell you he ran away because Friday night he overheard me asking them about his whereabouts that morning? I'm sorry. I shouldn't have meddled."

Ah, so she did want to discuss Chad. This did not make him feel any better. He made a vow right then. Never again would he involve a civilian in a case in any way. "Yes, Tom called and told me after I interviewed Chad at my office."

She glanced up at him, dismay darkening her blue eyes. "I feel awful. Like I caused—"

"Don't." He cut her off. "Chad's running away"—and he added silently, *maybe his setting a fire*—"wasn't your fault. I should never have spoken to you. It wasn't fair." His conscience prickled. It was hard to admit that he'd gone to Audra only partly to shield Chad from unwarranted gossip.

Because something about her drew him. Made him entertain thoughts about her he shouldn't even consider. In the past decade, he'd avoided women, putting all his efforts into his career and into burying his wild youth. But lately he'd grown to hate going home to an empty house every night. And certainly Audra was a woman any man would love to find waiting for him.

Not just any man, his conscience mocked him. *You.*

"When I tried to apologize to Chad, he said that you'd made it right," Audra said. "What does that mean?"

He forced himself back to reality. The recent scene with her uncle flashed in his mind. Audra looked—what? Unconvinced? Vulnerable? She looked as though she might be holding something back. Did she suspect someone else or was all this just his mind working overtime? Or was she recalling Ramsdel's calling him names? Did she believe any of the poison her uncle spewed around about him? She cast him one more uneasy glance. "Sheriff?" she prompted. "What did you say to Chad?"

He stuffed his hands into his pockets to keep from touching her arm to reassure her. "I told him that I talked to you to try to keep people from suspecting him. And again, I'm sorry I bothered you."

She sighed. "I only wish I could have actually helped." A gull swooped overhead, shrieking to its comrades. Carter, Audra, and Evie reached her café. People were already milling around the locked gate. Audra pulled the key out of her pocket. The hungry-looking customers parted to make way for them as she led him forward.

Audra unlocked the gate and Carter followed her in. He had to get his coffee, his alibi for following her to work. Audra must have come to church from here earlier because he could smell the already-brewed coffee. Behind the counter, she pulled on her apron and poured him a to-go cup of coffee. Leaving dollars on the counter, he nodded his thanks and headed away to his job.

"Bye, Sheriff!" Evie waved to him.

Waving in return, he left them, putting aside the memory of brushing Audra's fingers. He could not let himself become infatuated with Evie's pretty mother. Audra and little Evie deserved someone without a past, someone her family could accept. Someone better with more to offer her.

Feeling several layers of gloom settle over him, he trudged back to his Jeep. Another day to protect and defend. The only question was—how could he prevent another fire? Was that possible? Would there be another fire?

———

HE LAY ON HIS BED, enjoying the feeling of being fully rested, fully satisfied. He hadn't felt this good for a long time. The first two fires had come off just the way he'd planned. And that felt great. Now he just had to figure out who should be the target of fire number three. Easy choice. He grinned and felt even better. What type of trigger should he use this time?

———

CARTER HOVERED in the dark alley near Audra's café's back-yard where she was about done selling pizzas for the evening. Nearly a week had passed without a third fire. He didn't know whether to be relieved or not. He couldn't shake the feeling that this trouble had only begun. But this evening his overall anxiety for Winfield was superseded by a more immediate concern.

You shouldn't be here. But when he'd visited Tom at Shirley's this evening, he hadn't been able to refuse a request to deliver two messages—one from Evie and the other from Shirley. He hadn't missed the gleam in Shirley's eye. It was a matchmaking gleam. At thirty-six, he was well able to recognize it. *But that didn't stop you from coming here.* He'd wanted to come, hadn't been able to stay away any longer. He could at least be honest with himself.

Over the week, each morning, he'd given in to temptation and stopped to buy coffee from her. Each time something troubling had lurked in the depths of Audra's royal-blue eyes. So far he'd waited for her to broach whatever was bothering her. But he couldn't wait any longer. It might have to do with the fires. He had to find out what was troubling her.

Brent, Ramsdel's son, strolled out Audra's back door. He called over his shoulder, "See you tomorrow, Audra! Tell Evie I'm going to take her to the beach tomorrow."

Feeling something like a dieter caught with unwrapped chocolate in hand, Carter hung back in the shadows. *If you don't want to get her into trouble with her family, you shouldn't be here. This is the last time you give in to temptation. The last time. Get her to open up, tell the truth and then leave.*

"Hey, Brent!" Chad stepped out from the shadows around the streetlamp at the end of the alley.

Brent halted, turning to locate Chad in the dim light. "Oh, it's just you."

Carter groaned. Not now.

"We never settled our previous disagreement," Chad jeered, and then he rushed Brent.

"Stop that!" Audra shouted and came running out her back door.

"Stay out of this, Audra!" Brent yelled.

"That's right, stay out of this, Audra," Carter repeated, moving fast.

Chad punched Brent and the two teens went down hard.

Carter charged out of the shadows. He couldn't let Audra try to break up two teens fighting. Even at only fourteen, Chad and Brent were strong enough to hurt her if she got between them. "Freeze!" Carter called out. "It's the sheriff!"

The two guys were tangled together, punching and rolling around on the cracked asphalt. Carter bent down and dragged them apart by their collars. "Cool it! I mean it! You're disturbing the peace and if you don't stop it, I'll take you both in." Carter didn't want to contemplate Hal Ramsdel's reaction to his taking Brent into the station, but that couldn't be helped.

Both teens glared at him and tried fruitlessly to pull from his grip.

"Chad, you're supposed to be home by now, aren't you?" Carter challenged.

Chad swiped at dirt on his cheek. "What business is it of yours?"

"Because I like Shirley and I don't want her to be losing sleep over you. Don't you think you upset her enough by running away last week?" Carter went on without giving Chad a chance to answer. "Now head home and I'll be there to check up on you shortly." He let the kid loose and pushed him in the direction of Shirley's.

Then he let Brent pull himself from his grip.

"Don't touch me again." Brent glared.

"Don't make me." Carter nodded in the opposite direction from where Chad was walking. "Head on home and don't go near Chad again."

Brent grumbled under his breath but stalked away to his bike.

⸺

AUDRA STOOD IN HER BACKYARD, taken aback by the sudden violence.

Carter walked toward her. "Audra, are you all right? That was just kid stuff."

At the sound of his deep commanding voice, excitement rippled through her. But was followed by her uneasiness over her uncle's mental state . Her concern had begun after the argument between Carter and Hal at her place. It had dogged her all week and now it spoiled her sudden joy at seeing Carter here. She wouldn't bring it up. She had no proof that her uncle might be angry enough to do something to cause Carter trouble—only a feeling. Just because her uncle was upset all the time didn't mean he could have anything to do with the fires.

"I'm so glad you were here to stop them," Audra said, trying to sound composed. "I'm going to have to ask Tom and Shirley to have another talk with Chad about steering clear of Brent."

Carter hung back just beyond the light cast from the doorway. "It's just kid stuff," he repeated. "And I'll talk to Tom. It's too bad that Chad's father didn't lose custody of his son earlier. Chad wouldn't have this deep well of anger then."

"Why didn't anyone turn Doyle in for abuse?" Audra asked.

"My guess, Chad's dad is cagey and has nasty ways of getting even with anyone who crosses him."

The lingering anxiety pinched her again. She couldn't talk about her uncle. Not with Carter. Audra wrapped her arms around herself and half turned. "I have a little bit more to do before I leave. Thanks—"

"I came to deliver two messages—one from your daughter and one from Shirley." He still hung back as though he wouldn't be welcomed here.

His obvious hesitance to be seen at her door pricked her like a sticker weed. The memory of the awful scene last week between this man and her uncle still made her stomach lurch. And she resented it, which only irritated her more. What right did her uncle have to spew his venom about Carter?

The better memory intruded—the sweeter one from last

Sunday that had lightened her spirits all week—of him lifting Evie in his arms and making her little girl glow... She decided to follow her instincts. Her uncle was wrong, and she wouldn't go along with his self-destructive behavior. "Come in, Sheriff," she said with a sudden welcoming smile. She threw open the door for him.

He eased inside, his eyes searching hers. "Do you lock the door after you close up?"

She shut the door behind him. "Yes, I like the undisturbed quiet time after the day's rush." His presence trickled through her like warm maple syrup. In self-defense, though, she turned her back to him and went to work measuring out ingredients for the next morning's sweet rolls. "What were the two messages?" she asked in a businesslike tone.

"Well, first Evie told me to tell you 'Good night. Sleep tight.'" Carter's voice softened as he spoke her daughter's name.

This clutched at her heart. *He really cares about my little girl.* How she hated not to be at home to put Evie to bed herself. Unexpected guilt twisted inside her. But it had to be this way for Evie's sake. Then Audra stiffened her mother's heart against the obvious appeal of Carter bringing this message to her. "Thank you," she murmured.

"I... She's a great kid. But if you want me to step back..."

Audra swung around to face him. So he'd sensed her caution over his attention to Evie. But who was really important here—her Uncle Hal, the town gossips, or her innocent, loving daughter? The answer was easy. "Don't step back. I appreciate the attention you show Evie."

Audra's pulse thrummed at her own boldness. "You and Tom have been great for her. Before Tom moved into Shirley's as a boarder and then started dating her, Brent was the only male who showed Evie any attention. And until last fall when they moved north, that only happened at holidays and summers. Please don't stop. Evie thinks you're wonderful." She swallowed then, as breathless as if she'd just sprinted around the block twice.

They stood looking at each other. Audra's gaze then focused on his large, capable hands, strong but gentle. She recalled how he'd patted Evie's hair with such care.

"I don't want to give people any room for gossip."

His words pulled her back from her preoccupation. She shook her head. "People should know better."

He leaned back against her closed door. "I don't want to cause trouble for you."

There was nothing to say to this. People should know better, but how many did? She turned to her measuring cups, shutting out the flagrantly masculine image he made lounging against the door. "What was Shirley's message?"

"Your mother called and would like you to call her back."

This news sent an instant frost through her. How could she change her negative reaction whenever she was confronted with her mother? It wasn't right. But how could they get back to the way they should be? The thought nagged her. "Did Shirley say anything else?" she asked, outwardly cool.

"Not much. Your mom's up for the weekend and would like to hear from you."

"I wonder why she didn't call me here," Audra said, pointedly not looking at him. But it was happening again. His presence was filling up the space, making the room and her lungs feel smaller, tighter. Making her want to confide in him. Was she just jumping to conclusions about her uncle?

"Maybe your mother didn't want to take up your time while you were working."

"I suppose." Or maybe she was unhappy about Megan working here and wanted to vent. Audra cut off the babble of uncertainties over Megan and her mother that fizzed up inside her.

"Well, I'll be going then." Carter moved to leave. Audra turned to say good-bye. Her phone rang and after one ring, it went to the answering machine which played her recording: "Sorry, please call again or leave a message." She walked on toward the door to lock it.

A harsh and familiar voice came on after the beep, "Audra. Pick up."

Halfway to the door, she froze in place. Shocked. What would he be calling her about?

"Audra, I know you're there. Pick up."

She shook off the shock of hearing that voice and proceeded to the door. She had nothing to say to the caller and there was nothing she wanted to hear from him. "Sheriff, thanks for the messages," she said, ignoring the voice over the phone. "I have to get busy and put the ingredients in and set the dough machine timers."

"Audra, pick up. Aud—" The answering machine clicked off.

After glancing between the phone and her, the sheriff pursed his lips. "Is that something—"

"No, nothing." She cut him off. "Just an old acquaintance who wants a loan," she ad-libbed.

He didn't look convinced, but he left. Behind him, she clicked the dead bolt into place and then slipped the key into her pocket. The voice over the phone had sounded angry.

Audra switched on the radio to the oldies station and turned the volume up. "Forget it," she responded silently to the caller. "I'm not calling you back. Stay away from me."

Her mind turned to Shirley's message. Why had her mother called Shirley? Was this one of her mother's "I want to salve my conscience and act like I care about my daughter and my only granddaughter" calls?

Uncle Hal, Brent, Megan, now her mother. Maybe Audra was small for thinking this, but all of a sudden she felt as if she had way too much family and way too many of them were in Winfield.

The phone rang and the answering machine picked up. The same voice spoke again. Audra turned the volume of the radio even louder, drowning him out with Lesley Gore's classic, "It's My Party." Humming along, she took a deep steadying breath. The lingering apprehension about her uncle having something to do with the fires had become an itch she wanted to scratch. But it was just her overwrought imagination.

Chapter 5

The next day, Saturday morning swept in, carrying with it a fresh rush of coffee-deprived customers. By now Audra had become inured to sleep deprivation. Or maybe she'd become too sleepy to notice? The weekend crush of tourists was gratifying and she was pleased to see repeat business, a good indicator that her specialty coffees and baked goods were a success. Meanwhile, she'd decided her vague suspicions about her uncle were groundless. She was glad she hadn't said anything to Carter about them. But then there was the message Carter had delivered from her mother to call her. What did her mother want to say to her?

After the first wave of customers, she had turned back from starting another pot of fragrant flavored coffee, when her mother came walking up the flagstone path of Audra's Place. With a sudden pang, Audra's heart leaped and sped up. Would this be another one of their frozen, stilted meetings? *I don't want to feel this way about my mother, or act this way with her, Lord. Help me make things better between us.*

As usual, Megan was there busy wiping tables with Evie. Megan had said nothing this morning about their mother. Tall and slender as always, her mother wore a blue-and-white designer jogging outfit. Had her sister known their mother would be stopping by without giving Audra any warning? Audra braced herself.

"Good morning, Audra," her mother said when she reached the counter. "Since you didn't have a chance to call me back, I decided to drive in for a cup of coffee and a roll." Her mother's voice didn't betray anything—neither disappointment nor irritation over Audra not returning her call.

"Hello, Mother." Audra felt her face warming. "I was going to call you this morning when things calmed down. I got your message too late to call you last night." Which was true, but just barely. Audra waited for her mother to comment archly about Megan working for her.

Lois gazed around. "Your location is very good. I've always admired this house. I like the exterior color scheme you chose. It's just a bit out of the ordinary without being gaudy."

Her mother's approval of her combination of white, green, and blue was completely unexpected. For a moment, Audra was at a loss for words. Then she managed, "Thanks. Can I get you a coffee?"

"Yes, please. Just black. And one of those almond biscotti might be tasty."

Out of the corner of her eye, Audra saw Chad and Tom, both dressed in their work clothes, walk in through the gate. "Hey, Evie." Tom greeted her little girl with a friendly wave.

"Hi, Tom. Hi, Chad!" That was when Evie appeared to notice her grandmother's presence. She hurried along with the other two up to the counter. She looked up. "Hello, Grandmother Blair."

Her daughter's painfully polite tone was a fingernail on the chalkboard of Audra's nerves.

"Hello, Eve." Her mother smiled. "I see you have an Audra's Place apron just your size."

"Yes, I help my mama every morning. I wipe the tables and Auntie Megan carries the mugs to the kitchen and washes them."

Now the feathers would hit the fan. Waiting for her mother's reaction, Audra poured her coffee, mulling over her own reaction to her daughter interacting with her grandmother. Evie had approached her grandmother as if she were a visiting queen. Not the way Audra had always joyously greeted her own two grandmothers. Did her mother even notice this? Care about it? And what did Tom make of all this as he stood, watching, waiting his turn?

"That sounds like a good plan, Eve," her mother said with an approving nod.

The nod evidently encouraged Evie. As if wading into frigid water, she edged closer to her grandmother.

Tom ordered two mocha lattes to go. Audra began to concoct them, keeping an eye on the polite conversation that her mother was painstakingly pursuing with Evie. This was unprecedented.

Megan, her hair pulled into a high ponytail, strolled up. "Hi, Mom. What do you think of Audra's Place?"

Audra held her breath. Now it would come. Megan had issued an open invitation for a negative comment about Megan working for Audra.

"Good location and very appealing, almost like a European outdoor café." Their mother picked up the mug of steaming coffee. "So this is where you hurried off to this morning?" She lifted a professionally plucked eyebrow.

"Yeah, Evie's great at cleaning the tables, but she needs some help carrying the dishes."

Evie claimed Megan's hand and leaned against her.

With lips parted, Audra waited for one of her mother's usual cutting remarks.

Their mother sipped her hot coffee cautiously. "Well, Megan, I'm glad you're making yourself useful."

Audra's mouth snapped shut. Silently she added the espresso to Tom's lattes.

"But why couldn't you just tell me where you were going?" Her mother shook her head and sighed.

"I'm just a woman of mystery these days," Megan said with an airy lift of her hand.

Their mother turned to Audra. "I'm looking for someone to do some yard work. Old Charlie has retired at last. Can you recommend someone?"

Her mother's calm acceptance of Megan's presence still threw Audra off-balance. What had she asked? "I really—" Audra began.

"Audra, Chad might be able to do some yard work," Tom spoke up.

After a glance at Tom, her mother sent Audra a questioning look.

"I'm sorry. Mother, this is Tom Robson. He owns the repair garage here in town." Then Audra nodded toward Chad. "And Chad works for Tom."

"Yeah, I work for Tom," Chad sneered, "in between setting fires."

Audra blushed, embarrassed for Tom.

Tom shook Chad by the shoulder. "Chill. Mrs. Blair, I think Chad is just the person to do your yard work. I can't keep him as busy at my shop as I'd like to. He's too young to work on some of the stuff I deal with. Here's my card." Tom pulled one from his pocket. "Call me or Shirley Johnson—she's Chad's foster parent—and we'll set something up."

Chad made a sound of derision and turned away, muttering something about "rich summer people."

Audra felt sympathy for Chad and at the same time wanted to shake him.

"Thank you," her mother said. "I didn't expect to find someone so easily." She accepted the card from Tom's work-worn hands, but still held it as if it might be contaminated. "But what's this about fires?"

"Lois!" Hal's voice boomed over the chatter of Audra's customers.

Hail, hail, the family's all here. Audra groaned inwardly. She silently urged the frothy milk to come out of the machine faster. She didn't need Hal, Chad, and her mother all together in front of her counter. She finished concocting the two lattes and Tom handed her a bill.

"I'm glad you've come to see how well your daughter's doing." Hal launched his first salvo.

Lois greeted her brother, ignoring his jibe. "How do you like Winfield year-round, Hal?"

Audra gave Tom a few coins in change.

As Tom and Chad started to leave, Hal noticed Chad and gave the teen a black look.

"What're you looking at?" Chad taunted.

Tom shook Chad's shoulder again. "Stop looking for trouble. Come on. We have work to do." Tom drew Chad away with him down the flagstone path.

"Is there something I should know about that young man?" Lois turned to watch Chad leaving.

"He's been setting fires around town," Hal said.

"That's not proven," Audra said quietly, firmly. "I wish you wouldn't add to the gossip, Uncle Hal." She began making his usual morning order, a tall coffee with double cream. Unfortunately, seeing him argue with her mother reanimated her fear over her uncle's volatile state.

Her uncle ignored Audra. "Lois, it's about time you showed some support for your daughter."

Lois pursed her lips. "Let's not dig up the past, Hal. Audra has my complete support in her new venture. I think she'll be very successful."

She had her mother's complete support? Audra pondered this earthshaking news.

Hal disregarded Lois's comments. "It's time you started acting like Audra's mother, not some distant relation who doesn't care—"

"Hal, you never change," Lois snapped. "Do you ever listen to anyone but yourself?"

"Lois, do you ever think of anyone but yourself? The way you've treated Audra is awful. You should thank your lucky stars that you have your two daughters—"

"Hal, I grieved over losing Sarah, too, but Audra isn't Sarah, and I'm not you."

Audra listened to this exchange with growing unease. It was always the same, this bickering between her uncle and mother. At least, it had been ever since Audra's father and Sarah had died, and Evie was born. If it weren't so distressing, it would be droll, almost comical. She handed her uncle his cup.

He ignored her except to hand her two bills. "Lois, you just don't get it, do you?" He shook his head and marched away like the admiral of the fleet.

"And he wonders why both his wives left him," her mother murmured, gazing after him, and then turned to Audra. "Is there anything I should know about this Chad? Or is that all in my brother's twisted mind?"

My brother's twisted mind. Maybe Audra wasn't alone in worrying about her uncle's mental state. Not meeting her mother's eyes at first, she wiped the glass counter. "Chad is Shirley's foster son. He did have a record of setting fires before he came to live with her last year. But he's done nothing recently." Audra met her mother's eyes. "There were two fires last weekend—"

"I know. I read the local paper last night. Do you think Chad set them?"

"No, I don't," Audra stated, keeping eye contact with her mother. "The sheriff questioned Chad but didn't charge him. Brent and Chad are at odds. I think he's just a convenient suspect for Uncle Hal." *And everyone else.*

Her mother nodded. "Very well. Your uncle has never been a good judge of character. How much do I owe you?"

"Nothing." The question sizzled embarrassingly through Audra. "My pleasure."

With the coffee and biscotti in one hand, Lois slipped a five-dollar bill from her pocket and onto the counter. Before Audra could object, she moved away. Over her shoulder, she called, "Oh, by the way, when can Eve spend an afternoon with me?"

Audra opened her mouth but no words came forth. Her mother had never invited Evie to visit her alone. Audra swallowed, swallowed again. "When would you like her?"

"How about Wednesday afternoon? Megan can bring her home for lunch."

Audra nodded, feeling as if she had missed a step while running downstairs. What was going on with her mother?

With a wave, Lois turned away. Halfway down the flagstone path, she paused to have a word with her granddaughter. Evie beamed and Lois patted her cheek. Motioning Evie to join her, Lois sat at a table to drink her coffee. After Lois finished her light breakfast and departed, Evie ran up to Audra. "Mama, Grandmother Blair says I'm coming to visit her! On Wednesday! Don't forget, okay?"

Audra took pleasure in her daughter's excitement. Were things about to change between her mother and her? Her pleasure dimmed as her fears over who might be setting the fires and why prickled the hair on the back of her neck. Maybe she was crazy to suspect Hal. But the worry tugged at her.

ARRIVING AT THE THIRD fire of the tourist season, Carter watched the gray-and-black smoke billowing skyward. And did a slow burn, too. Over two weeks had passed since the first two fires. He'd dared to hope a third wouldn't occur. Now in the early-June evening, Carter stood back as the firefighters finished putting down the fire on the grounds of the Blair lake-side summer home.

Fortunately, the target of the fire had been the garden shed and not the main house. Carter glanced to the rear deck, which overlooked Lake Superior, and glimpsed a woman, watching the firefighters. That must be Lois Blair, Audra's widowed mother. She wore white slacks and a navy-blue blouse and stood aloof with her arms crossed. How would she react to this? After all, Ramsdel was her brother. Anything was possible. Dread slipped down into his stomach.

"That's it," the local fire chief called to Carter. "We've soaked everything. Let it cool and then you can begin your investigation."

Carter waved his thanks. He then turned and headed toward Lois. He needed to get information from her first. Another factor intruded on this investigation. The more he tried to stay away, the more incidents drew him to Audra and her family.

Now he was here to question her mother about a fire. From Tom and from general comments he'd heard around town over the past seven years since Audra came to live with Shirley, Carter knew that there was some kind of breach between Audra and her mother. All this zipped through his mind as he approached the tall slender woman. He mounted the steps up to the deck. "Mrs. Blair, I'm Sheriff Harding."

"Sheriff." She offered him a cool, manicured hand. "Please sit down." She motioned him toward one of the two nearest green-and-white-striped padded chairs.

Carter settled into one as Lois sat in the other. He pulled

out a notebook. "Mrs. Blair, I promise I'll make a thorough investigation of this fire."

"Do you think the same person has set all three?"

He shrugged. "It's too early to tell. The three fires have nothing in common except that all three have been set in Winfield."

"That young man, Chad Keski, did some yard work for me here this afternoon. I believe he's set fires in the past?"

Chad being on scene here was unwelcome news to Carter. But he couldn't avoid the unpleasant. "Do you know that he had something to do with setting your shed on fire?"

Lois Blair eased back in her chair. "I don't know. But I do know that he evidently didn't want to do the simple mowing and raking job for me. That's all I wanted him to attempt his first time here. I decided I'd better do the flower beds myself."

"If he didn't want to do it, why did he?"

"I think that man, Tom..." Her brows drew together.

"Tom Robson, my stepfather?"

"He's your stepfather?"

Carter nodded.

"I guess that's how it is in a small town." She waved a dismissive hand. "Tom's your stepfather, Shirley Johnson's sweetheart, and Chad's employer." She paused. "I think Tom pushed Chad into doing my yard work."

Carter let the part about Tom being Shirley's sweetheart go by. "Why would Tom make Chad work here?"

"I don't know. You know your stepfather better than I do." The woman shrugged. "But I got the feeling it was something along the line of 'Idle hands are the devil's workshop.' Tom said he didn't have enough work to keep this Chad busy. My daughter did tell me that Chad had set fires before he'd come to be Shirley Johnson's foster son."

"Yes, that's right." He didn't like acknowledging this but it was, after all, common knowledge.

"However, you don't think he's the one setting these new fires?" Her eyes narrowed at him.

"I don't have any evidence linking Chad to either of the two fires." Or anyone else. "It's too early to say what I'll find out from this crime scene. Now, is there anyone other than Chad that you can think of that would have motive and/or opportunity to set this fire?"

She pondered this, looking past him to the blue of Lake Superior rippling about two hundred feet behind him. "I've been in and out all day. I was here when Chad came, and I stayed while he did the work. And then I left again, had to run an errand in town. Could it have just been an accident?" she continued. "I smelled tobacco on Chad. Could he have just discarded a match or cigarette in some dry grass or leaves and it took time for it to ignite? That's something a teenager would do."

"That might be possible." But too much to hope for. "Anyone angry at you?"

Mrs. Blair gave a dry chuckle. "Only my brother, Hal, but then I don't think he really likes anyone but Audra."

Carter didn't know what to make of this sardonic comment. Evidently Hal Ramsdel and his sister didn't get along. But who did Ramsdel get along with? Ramsdel might dote on Audra, but from what Carter had observed, she didn't appreciate it. "No one else with motive or opportunity?" he repeated.

"Well, as I said, I was gone. The shed sits back from the road and my property is wooded. Anyone could come from the beach or road and if they were cautious, no one would see them. Plus I don't have any neighbors very near. In fact, a jogger on the beach reported the fire on her cell phone." She shrugged.

So it was as bad as he'd expected. No obvious suspect. He rose. "Mrs. Blair, I'm going to start my investigation now. My deputy, Trish Franklin, may show up here in the future to do a follow-up. Please leave everything as it is until I tell you we've collected all possible evidence."

"Of course." She nodded, dismissing him. "I'll be calling my insurance company, but I'll wait on you before doing anything else."

Carter strode toward his Jeep to get out his gear and begin combing the remains of the Blair garden shed for clues. Equal parts irritation and eagerness surged inside him. The last thing he'd wanted was another fire. But this did provide him an opportunity to find clues to solve these cases. *A clue, just something to follow up. That's all I ask.*

———

AT THE SOUND OF A KNOCK on Audra's rear kitchen door, she jerked to a halt. Alone, she was nearly done cleaning up after another Sunday evening of pizza-making. Earlier this evening just before Brent had arrived, she'd forced herself to call the sheriff and leave him a message to call her. But had he come instead? She stared at the door, her thoughts streaming fast in her mind. Over a week had passed since her mother's garden shed had been set on fire.

Each day had increased two urges she resisted. The first was her desire to put into words the idea that her uncle might do something as irrational as start fires. But wasn't that ridiculous? Yet more and more her uncle seemed to be a fuse easy to light. But she couldn't really see him setting fires at such odd places, could she? The second desire was to steer clear of the sheriff—her uncle played into this too, but this wasn't ridiculous. Her uncle's hatred of Carter was all too real, and irrational.

Finally the urge to find out who waited outside overcame her. Hoping the sheriff had come, she moved forward. Of course, he probably wouldn't tell her anything specific, but she couldn't put off seeing him any longer. Or maybe her nasty caller had come... Fear came, a single cold wet finger down her spine. She halted. "Who is it?"

"It's the sheriff."

Inside her, sudden relief tripped over tenseness, and the two tangled together. She wanted to see the sheriff. She probably shouldn't see him. She unlocked the door and opened it wide. "Thank you for coming." Her throat was dry. Her heart beat like a stammering child. Carter was in uniform as usual, but without his hat that often masked his green eyes. And for a moment his blatant masculinity held her in place.

⸻

"I WAS PASSING BY AND thought I might as well just stop in instead of calling." Carter didn't meet Audra's eyes as this altered version of the facts slipped out of his mouth. He could have called her. But instead, he'd parked his Jeep behind Shirley's and walked here so he could escort Audra home. He had no business wanting to walk her home through the quiet moonlit alley, but here he was. "What did you want to discuss?"

She took off her apron and hung it up. Underneath, she wore a light pink T-shirt and figure-hugging blue jeans. She turned away, rinsed out a washcloth, and began wiping down the already clean-looking counter. He followed her every move, unable to hide how she captivated him. Fortunately, she was avoiding eye contact too.

"How is the investigation of my mother's fire coming?" she asked.

Disappointment flared inside him, disintegrating his unspoken hope that Audra wanted to see him as much as he craved seeing her again. The fire. He should have known it was the investigation that prompted her call. Of course. What else? Certainly not a desire to see him again.

"The investigation of the crime scene is finished," he said. *Finished. But a complete bust.*

Three times, he'd gone over every inch of the charred remains of the shed and every inch of the yard and so had Trish. He'd come up with the fact that the fire had been ignited with a simple long-burning fuse, buried among lawn debris and nearby gasoline-soaked rags. Nothing more. Nothing that matched the modus operandi of the first two fires. And nothing to follow up. The third handful of pennies he'd found there had not helped, either.

"And you still don't have any clear suspect?"

"No." He considered her. She looked ill at ease, very ill at ease. "Why do you ask?" He spoke in a measured tone.

She rinsed out the cloth again, washed her hands, and then turned slowly toward him. "I've been uneasy..."

"About?" He waited.

"About my uncle," she muttered, staring down at her feet.

He followed her gaze. She was wearing thick-soled turquoise sandals that tied around her ankles. He became fascinated with her small toes peeping out from the colorful cloth toe. He forced his eyes up. "What about your uncle?"

She folded her arms. "It's nothing concrete. Just a feeling I have that he's near a...a breakdown of some kind." She cast him a covert glance. "You know why he and Brent moved north, don't you?"

"I've heard rumors. Why don't you tell me?" He rested a shoulder against the wall.

The phone rang and the answering machine picked up, reciting her message. Audra looked unnecessarily alarmed. "I'm done here. Why don't you walk me home?" She nearly pushed him toward the door as if fearing another message.

What's going on with the phone, Audra?

She switched off the lights. The answering machine shut off and the caller hung up. Her shoulders relaxed but she still moved toward the door. Carter stepped out into the dim light as she locked the dead bolt on the door. The deep twilight of the summer, a lingering glimmer of daylight still on the horizon, closed around them. Street lamps shone at each end of the block, leaving the middle in veiling shadow. They started walking side by side.

Should he ask her why her phone ringing caused this quick retreat? Did it have something to do with the last time he'd heard that angry voice demanding Audra pick up? He tried to think of a way to ask this diplomatically and failed. He waited, but when she said nothing, he prompted, "So why did your uncle come north?"

"He and his second wife, Brent's mother, broke up a year ago." Audra's voice was quiet, subdued, concerned. "The divorce was messy and Uncle Hal had to sell stocks and property at just the wrong time for the settlement."

"So he couldn't afford two homes anymore?"

"That's right."

"Why did he choose to come to Winfield?"

"I think it's something like making a fresh start. He took his insurance sales licensing tests and put his remaining capital into the agency here."

"Okay." He considered her comments. His footsteps crunched loud on the gritty pavement while hers made a soft padding sound. "Are you telling me you think that after all this, he's headed for some kind of...breakdown?" he finished, using her word.

"He's always been outspoken and opinionated."

Carter could think of a few more pithy ways to put this.

"But it's worse now," she explained earnestly. "He's just so emotional about everything these days. His every response is over the top. It's like he's spoiling for a fight with someone. All the time."

This was not news to him. "Where is this leading, Audra?" Her distress broke over him in waves. He wanted to reach out and help her in some way.

"I'm...I know this'll sound nuts, but I was wondering if he could have something to do with these fires."

"Your uncle?" Her words, so unexpected, nearly floored him.

"I know. I think I'm crazy too."

"No. I...no...why do you think he might be involved?"

She hesitated, walking slower.

He waited, matching her gait.

"I probably am crazy," she mumbled. She made a sound like a cat hissing. "When I think of my uncle, I don't really see him lurking in alleys setting fires. But he...carries such anger and such a grudge against you."

Carter made the connection. "You think he might be doing this to cause me trouble now that I'm sheriff?"

"I know it sounds stupid, doesn't it?" She gazed up at him, her large eyes luminous in the low light.

He fought to keep his mind on the topic at hand. "Not stupid, really. Just unsubstantiated."

"I feel like an idiot telling you this." She stopped walking and faced him. "But I've been so stressed about him..."

"It's understandable." He touched her shoulder. "But I doubt your uncle is involved."

"I feel better hearing you say that." She took a deep breath. "And I'm concerned about Brent. My uncle's just so agitated all the time."

You've got that right. He dropped his hand but moved closer as if supporting her. He didn't say anything. What could he say?

For the rest of the block, they walked along in silence. Carter listened to the night sounds—muffled voices in the distance, the lapping of waves against the wharf nearby. But the woman beside him dominated the quiet night, tempting him to focus only on her.

Audra's voice finally broke their silence. "You don't have any suspects yet for the fire at my mother's?"

He contemplated the clear, starry sky. "Since he'd been at the property that day, I questioned Chad." Carter could tell her that because it was common knowledge, no doubt. He didn't tell her that another stack of pennies had been found under all the debris. Pennies were the only link between all three fires. The coins were always blackened by the fire, so it wasn't someone leaving them after the fact. But pennies? The fire-setter had a strange sense of humor.

They started up the last block to Shirley's. Carter didn't want the walk to end. In spite of the heavy topic they'd discussed, he felt more at ease than he had for days. Audra had that effect on him; she relaxed him in one way and sparked tension in another. He had no doubts about her goodness. Her corn-silk-blond hair captured the moonlight. He wished she'd worn it down.

As if hearing his thoughts, she unclipped it and let it fall to her shoulders. She shook her head and ran her fingers through the long golden strands, each one highlighted by moonlight. He imagined letting his own hands slide in after hers. *No way. Stop.* He needed to take captive his attraction toward her. He would not be touching Audra Blair's hair any time soon. Probably never.

But then she drew a little nearer to him. He inhaled the fragrance of flowers from her. They were alone. She was so close and it was dark. He drifted closer to her. Could he possibly be feeling the same kind of pull toward him? Improbable. Unknowable.

He let her lead him to Shirley's roughed-in new back steps and shell of a porch. The smell of unfinished pinewood surrounded them. Turning to face him, she halted on the top step, which put them at the same height, face-to-face, nose-to-nose. "Carter," she murmured.

"Audra."

The fraction of an inch between them vibrated with awareness. Her lips parted slightly. He heard her inhale. He could barely breathe. As if having a mind of its own, his head dipped lower and then his lips were only a whisper away from hers.

She sighed into his mouth, and the warm puff snipped the last thread of his control. His lips brushed hers. She didn't move. Encouraged, he closed his eyes and let the kiss begin in earnest. Her lips were just as soft and honey-sweet as he'd imagined.

A nearby door flapped open. "You mangy cat, get out and good riddance!" It was Florence next door, letting her infamous tomcat out for the night.

Carter pulled back, steadying Audra with a hand at her elbow.

"Evening, Sheriff! Audra!" Florence crowed for all the neighborhood to hear. "It's a lovely full moon tonight, so romantic, isn't it?"

Chapter 6

The next evening, Monday, her only night off, Audra sat with Evie beside her at Shirley's long dining room table. She had expected to share the meal only with the other three who lived at Shirley's house—Tom, Chad, and Evie. But their hostess had surprised her by inviting Carter to join them. Shirley sat at the head of the table, Tom at the foot and Chad next to Carter across from Audra.

Beaming from the head of the table, Shirley asked Tom to offer grace. Everyone bowed their heads. Tom thanked God for bringing them all together for a meal. Audra tried to concentrate, but awareness of Carter churned through her. Whenever she thought about the kiss last night, her pulse tried to run away with her.

Suddenly came the sound of the back screen door opening and slamming and then a voice called from the kitchen. "Shirley!"

It was Florence.

Audra stared down at her plate. After last night, Florence had moved to the top of the list of the two people Audra least wanted to face. The other person was Carter, Audra's new temptation. And now they were both here. Another horrid thought blossomed in Audra's mind. What if Florence made some comment in front of Evie about last night's kiss? How would she handle that?

"We're in the dining room," Shirley called out.

In a white Proud Native American T-shirt and jeans, Florence sashayed through the doorway from the kitchen. "Oh, you're eating," she said in an unconvincing tone of surprise.

"Why don't you join us, Florence?" Shirley stood up and, from the carved sideboard, began setting another place beside Evie.

Tom grinned at her. "Your timing is impeccable, as always, Florence."

Florence pointed her long index finger at Tom. "You should know better than to stand outside my window grilling chicken."

Shirley chuckled as she squeezed her neighbor's shoulder. "You're quite welcome, Florence. Always. You know that. Come on, now. Tom was just offering grace."

Florence sat down. They all bowed their heads again. Tom continued thanking God, naming each of them and asking for blessings for each of them. Audra tried to think of a way to communicate to Florence not to let Evie know about the kiss. But nothing came to mind.

"Mama," Evie said, nudging Audra's shoulder, "Tom said, 'Amen.' Look up."

Audra looked up, right into Carter's tanned face. As she recalled his lips brushing hers, she glanced away. Her face and neck flamed and there was nothing she could do about it. Shirley gave her a knowing glance. Florence chuckled and winked. Rattled, Audra dipped a large spoon into the vat of mashed potatoes, her daughter's favorite food, and put a healthy mound on Evie's plate.

"Mama, don't you want some, too?"

Audra realized that she'd just passed the mashed potatoes to Tom without taking any. "I'm not very hungry," she said lamely.

"Yes, sometimes when we stand on the back porch in the moonlight, things happen that can take a person's appetite away." Brimming with obvious mischief, Florence helped herself to the mashed potatoes before passing them to Tom.

Audra sizzled with embarrassment and remembrance. Florence's words brought it all back, every sensation of Carter's kiss. She couldn't recall any kiss that had wound its way through her so completely, extinguishing any chance of denial.

Audra accepted the tray of chicken and served some to Evie and to her own plate. *Act normal*, she chastised herself.

But it was hard with a grinning Florence staring at Carter. Would Florence content herself with the amusement of teasing Audra about the kiss? What did Carter think of Florence's not-so-subtle gibes?

The serving bowls and platter finally made the rounds of the table and Audra managed to fill hers and Evie's plates. Couldn't this summer just calm down?

"Mama," Evie said, spooning up some mashed potatoes, "Grandma Lois is going to take me shopping tomorrow afternoon."

Audra realized she hadn't yet taken a bite of anything. Intensely conscious of Carter's every move and Florence's vigilance, she picked up her fork. "Shopping?" Her mother wanted to take Evie shopping? What next?

Evie nodded, her head bobbing. "We're going to shop for some pretty yarn. I can pick out any kind I want and then

Grandma Lois is going to teach me how to knit a scarf to keep me warm this winter." Evie was nearly bouncing in her seat with delight. When had Grandmother Blair become Grandma Lois?

"That sounds lovely, Evie," Shirley said. "What color do you think you'll like?"

"I don't know. Grandma Lois says I should wait and see. She's taking me to a special yarn shop in Ashford."

"There's a nice new bridal shop in Ashford, I hear," Florence said, evidently needling Audra.

Audra realized then she hadn't yet replied to Evie. She caught herself just before she addressed her as "Baby." "Honey, I think that's wonderful. Grandma Lois taught me how to knit when I was about your age, too." Her traitorous eyes then drifted over to Carter.

CARTER CAUGHT HIMSELF looking at Audra again. He should have declined Shirley's invitation.

That's right, his conscience taunted. *Last night you certainly gave Florence and probably the rest of the neighborhood grist for the gossip mill for months.*

He pushed this aside and took another bite of the charcoal-grilled chicken. Last night, he'd been so caught up with being with Audra that he hadn't pressed her about why she rushed him out of her kitchen just because her phone rang. Who was calling her that she didn't want to talk to? He needed to get her to confide in him. Angry phone calls could be a prelude to more damaging, more serious nastiness.

With a loud bang, Shirley's front door hit the wall of the foyer. Instantly Carter was up on his feet and met Chad's dad, Doyle, in the doorway to the hall. "Where's that Johnson woman?" Doyle shouted.

Carter blocked Doyle from entering the dining room. "Get out of here, Keski. You can't just barge into a private home—"

"I gotta right to look after my kid—"

Yeah, we all know how well you looked after him.

"That Johnson woman has no right making my boy do yardwork for some rich summer——." The epithet Keski used hit Carter the wrong way.

With his shoulder, Carter forced Doyle back toward the door.

Doyle's tirade continued, undeterred. "That blowhard Ramsdel had the nerve to call me and tell me you questioned my kid about setting fire to his sister's lousy shed!" Doyle let fly a string of insults against Hal and Lois.

Carter grabbed Doyle by the shirtfront and rammed him back toward the wide-open door. "You weren't invited here. Leave now, or I'm running you in for disturbing the peace!"

"I hope my kid did set that fire! It would show he has some guts!"

Carter propelled Doyle out through the screen door.

Doyle stumbled and nearly fell. He vaulted down Shirley's front steps and out to his rattletrap truck where a blonde with a lot of hair waited.

Sudden adrenaline slammed through Carter. His lungs heaved. He turned and marched back toward his chair. At the same time, he heard feet pounding, retreating up Shirley's staircase. Back in the dining room, he noted that Chad had vacated his place.

Having risen, Shirley slumped back into her chair, looking shaken. Tom hurried to her side. "That man..." Shirley said and propped her forehead in her hand. "That man. Why did he have to come back to town? He upsets Chad. I was making progress and then Doyle has to bring his sorry self back to Winfield."

Florence was standing beside Shirley, patting her back.

"Mama, that man scared me." Evie huddled close to her mother. Audra folded her daughter into her arms.

Carter knelt down beside them. He rested his hand on Evie's trembling back. "Evie, I won't let him hurt you. Or anyone."

The little girl peered around her mother at him. "But what if you wasn't here? That bad man might have hurt Nana Shirley. He hurt Chad."

Carter patted her back. "That won't happen. And Tom is here even if I'm not."

"But you're the sheriff!" Evie objected.

"Evie," Tom said, "don't be scared. If that bad man shows his face here again, I'll take care of him. I wouldn't let him hurt Shirley or you. And neither would Chad."

"And if you yell loud enough, Evie, I'll come over loaded for bear," Florence added, her expression fierce.

Evie nodded but with a doubtful look and then she touched Carter's hand. "Thanks, Sheriff."

"Yes, thanks, Carter," Shirley echoed.

Audra smiled over at him, her lower lip trembling.

Curse the man for upsetting everyone. Being so near Audra, Carter caught the same flowery fragrance as last night. With effort, he stopped himself from leaning over to kiss her again. He squeezed her shoulder instead. Then he eased away and returned to his chair.

"Let's not let Doyle ruin this good meal." He stared down at his plate and made himself pick up his knife and fork. *And very soon, Audra, you're going to tell me who those phone calls are from. And then I'm going to take care of whoever it is.*

———

EARLY ON TUESDAY MORNING, just after four o'clock, Audra hugged her sweater around herself in the chilly morning dampness. As she hurried down the alley on her way to work, the sleepy sun glowed hazy pink just beneath the horizon. She and Tom had set out together. His garage was only one block down from Shirley's and her place was three blocks. Usually he hadn't even risen when she left, but he had a rush job to get done today. Just as they'd left the backyard together, Shirley had called him back to ask him a question.

So Audra hurried on alone. Soon, from behind her through the peaceful gloom, she heard Tom's footsteps. Then they stopped and she heard the jingle of his keys and the creak of the gate of his back fence of his business yard. The clear morning air and quiet sleeping town caused sounds to be amplified. She neared the cross street. And then she heard it— the sudden explosive Bang and Swoosh.

She swung back. And screamed. Through the mist, flames poured, roared out of Tom's back door. "Tom!" she shrieked, "Tom!" Then she was running toward the blaze. She threw herself through the gate. Black smoke obscured her vision. She choked. Another loud pop and another. Glass shattering. More explosions? Were they inside or out here in the yard? "Tom!" Strangled by the smoke, she coughed.

Bending low trying to get beneath the roiling smoke, she moved forward. Then she saw Tom face-up, flattened on the ground, his shirt on fire!

She screamed and propelled herself forward onto her knees beside him. She beat the flames with her hands. Screaming. More popping sounds and then another boom!

The force of the explosion slapped her to the ground. The sound of flames roared in her ears. In the distance, the siren summoning the firefighters wailed. She wavered back onto her knees and slapped out the last flames on his shirt. "Tom! Tom!" She shook him. He moaned but didn't answer.

God! God! Please help! "We have to get out, Tom!"

Still no reply.

Coughing, she staggered to her feet, grabbed Tom's wrists, and began tugging his dead weight. Audra felt the scorching heat on her arms and face, smelled Tom's burned flesh. A siren continued over the roar of the fire. Was help coming?

"Tom! Tom!" It was Shirley somewhere in the smoke.

"Help me!" Audra shouted but had to stop as paroxysms of gagging suffocated her.

Then Shirley was beside her, helping her pull Tom to safety. The two women dragged Tom through the gate and into the alley. Audra stumbled to her knees. Florence was suddenly there helping her up, tugging her farther away from the inferno.

"Is he all right?" Audra gasped through a raw throat. "Is Tom all right?"

———

CARTER BLINKED HIS EYES, awaking abruptly. His cell phone on the bedside table was vibrating as it rang. The luminous bedside clock announced the time as 4:24 a.m. He picked up, rubbing his scratchy eyes. "Hello."

"Sheriff, I hate to have to tell you." Carter recognized the voice of the night dispatcher, a young woman. He'd gone through school with her older sister. "But it's your stepfather's—"

Icy fear zipped up his spine. "What?" He sat up and scrubbed his face with his hand. "What is it?"

"Your stepdad's shop is on fire. The firefighters are on their way. I got the 911 call."

Spikes of shock stabbed him. Another fire! And at Tom's! "On my way." He hung up. Hustling into his clothes, he raced out of the house to his Jeep. His stepdad wouldn't be at the shop this early in the morning, so he wouldn't be in danger. But his heart pounded anyway.

How much damage would this fourth fire cause to Tom's shop? It was only a block from Shirley's. What if it spread to the homes across the alley? With his siren blaring, he sped down the two-lane highway into town, his sheriff thoughts vying with his private concern for his stepdad's business.

Long before he arrived, he saw the flames and billowing black smoke. *Dear God, don't let anyone get hurt. Protect our firefighters.* When he reached Tom's block, he parked his Jeep and ran toward the fire truck. Flames had fully engulfed the fifties vintage gas station where his stepdad fixed engines and machinery of all kinds. The volunteer fire company in their bright yellow-and-black gear was working hoses, trying to contain the fire and put it out.

Black smoke rolled into the predawn gray. Carter stiffened in the cloying early-morning dampness and looked around for Tom. Surely he'd have come here as soon as he heard the sirens. "Tom! Tom!" He jogged along the alley toward a crowd of onlookers. People in robes stood back in nearby yards watching the firefighters' progress. Carter shoved his chilled hands up under his arms, scanning the crowd for Tom. Why couldn't he find Tom?

"Over here, Carter!"

Carter recognized Audra's shaky voice. Up ahead, she leaned against Florence under a maple tree in the backyard of Wilma's bed-and-breakfast. He sprinted to her and opened his arms. "Are you hurt? What happened?" He scanned her pale shocked face, smeared with tears and soot.

She moved into Carter's arms. "Oh, Carter, I heard it go off." She began coughing.

Like a needle puncturing a balloon, her words released his pent-up fear about more fires. "What? What went off?" He held her against him, resisting the urge to shake the words from her. Her trembling shook him and then she began sobbing into his shirt.

"Are you hurt?" He loosened his hold and looked down at her. Carter caught the smell of Audra's singed hair.

"Her hands are burned," Florence informed him. "She swallowed smoke, too. I think that's what makes her keep coughing. I left Chad taking care of Evie back at Shirley's."

"Carter," Shirley called, "Tom's over here!"

In the smoky haze, Carter pulled Audra along with him. "Is he hurt?" he asked in disbelief.

Shirley was kneeling beside Tom, who was lying face-up on the grass. "Yes," she said. "But we got him out before the fire got way worse. And Wilma here had enough sense to spray him with the garden hose. He must have been very close when the fire ignited. I was in my kitchen when I heard the explosion."

"Why was he here so early? He doesn't open till eight o'clock." Carter released Audra to Florence's care again and dropped down to the dewy grass at his stepfather's side. Tom's face showed reddened, blackened skin, blisters, and black soot. The remnants of his shirt, soaked with water, were charred in front and stuck to his chest. "Tom, it's me, Carter." He could barely force out the words. Who had done this to Tom? He checked Tom's pulse and found it weak and thready. Fear rose higher.

His stepfather twisted slightly, moaning, but said nothing.

"I wish the ambulance would get here," Shirley fretted.

Carter jumped to his feet and called to the volunteers swarming around the billowing fire. "We need help here! Injured man needs help."

One of the volunteers hurried over. He took one look and said, "He's going into shock."

"Yes, and this woman might be too," Carter said to the volunteer, motioning toward Audra, "You better check her for burns and for shock. There was more than one explosion. She may have a concussion."

The volunteer nodded. "Sheriff, I'll run to the truck and get a pack of those foil blankets."

Shirley moaned. "When I got here, Audra was already in the middle of it, trying to drag Tom out." Shirley began weeping. "She'd been on her way to work." She looked skyward and shouted, "Where is that ambulance?"

Within minutes the volunteer returned with the pack and ripped it open. Both Carter and the volunteer firefighter whom he now recognized as a local carpenter pulled free two of the foil blankets and wrapped them around Tom and Audra. People began moving closer to the fire and Carter waved them back. "Back! Back!"

As he paced up the alley, shepherding people back to a safe distance, Carter wanted three things: to get Audra and Tom to the hospital in Ashford, question the fire chief and any eyewitnesses—all in the same instant. Dawn brightened around them, breaking through the smoke and mist.

Noise from the firefighters continued. There were three more bangs. Carter stared up at black smoke filling the alley, straining skyward, blocking the dawn. People stopped moving forward and a few ran away.

Another police car sped up the alley and rocked to a halt. Trish scrambled out and ran toward him. "Who's hurt?" she called out over the din from the fire crew.

"My stepfather!" Carter shouted in reply. He pressed a hand to his own forehead, throbbing as if it were about to explode. *Why can't I figure this out, God? Stop these fires?*

Carter kept watch on Audra and Tom from a distance as he controlled the crowd with Trish's help while the firefighters battled on. They finally managed to get the fire under control. The fire chief located Carter in the crowd and halted in front of him. "This was one tough fire. So much grease, gasoline, et cetera on site. We're going to be here a few more hours before it's completely out."

A distinctive siren in the distance interrupted him. EMTs from Ashford had arrived at last. The ambulance pulled up a safe distance from the smoldering fire. Carter motioned them over. "We have two injured here. This woman, Audra Blair, and the man on the ground, Tom Robson."

The EMTs swarmed around Tom first and then Audra. The ambulance and the fire trucks were backlit by the pink dawn. One EMT hurried along beside Carter as he carried Audra toward the ambulance. The other two lifted Tom onto a rigid stretcher. "How serious is he?" Carter asked over his shoulder. "He's my stepdad."

"He's in shock. He's suffered first and second-degree burns on his chest, face, and hands. If you have to stay with the fire, is there any other family that can come with him?"

Carter looked at Shirley.

"I can't go, Carter. I've got Evie to take care of. Only Chad's with her right now. Can't you go with both of them?"

Carter was torn. "I should stay and start investigating as soon as the firefighters put out the blaze." But Trish was more than capable of securing the crime scene. Plus he couldn't do anything here until the firefighters were finished and things cooled. That wouldn't be for hours. Tom and Audra needed him.

"Trish, take charge here!" Carter followed the EMTs. "After the firefighters are done, lock this crime scene up tight and post someone to guard it. I'm going to follow the ambulance."

"Yes, sir!" Trish jogged toward the fire chief.

Carter hurried to his Jeep. Now that the ambulance was taking Audra and Tom for treatment, his mind could turn to the crime. Audra had said, "I heard it go off." Shirley had heard something explode. He'd heard some small explosions himself. So that meant this was not just a case of a machine shop filled with greasy tools catching on fire.

Definitely another arson, perhaps a booby trap like the first.

And this time people had been hurt, and not just any people. They were two of the most important people in the world to Carter. *Someone is going to pay for this. And soon.* Then another thought stopped him. With this fire, was someone trying to get at him by attacking Tom?

Chapter 7

That evening, Carter strode up the quiet corridor of the small hospital in Ashford. Shirley walked beside him with a paper shopping bag in hand. "I still can't believe this happened," she murmured.

He reached out and squeezed her arm just as they arrived at Tom's room.

Tom was sitting up in bed. When he saw them, he switched off the TV. "Shirley! Son!" He opened his bandaged arms, making the IV tubes hooked to his left arm sway. Shirley hurried forward and kissed him.

Carter stood back and surveyed his stepdad. Tom's reddened face was covered with bandages and salve and his chest was bandaged like his arms. Carter had a hard time drawing breath. *Why can't I find any evidence to arrest this arsonist?*

"Carter," Tom said, his voice low and grating.

Carter walked to the other side of the bed and gently took his stepdad's hand. "You look like you've been through a war."

"Yeah, and our side lost." Tom managed a one-sided grin. "Carter, I know you feel like this is all your fault," he said, "but it's not. It's the fault of whoever is setting these fires. Not you."

Tom's kind words stung Carter's eyes with saltwater. He blinked it away.

Tom went on before Carter could reply. "Did you find any useful clues at my place?"

"Our arsonist is getting better," Carter admitted.

"Why don't you go find Audra and tell her what you discovered," Shirley suggested, "and what's happened since she left Winfield this morning? I can fill Tom in on everything you told me." She turned to Tom. "I know you'll say it isn't necessary, but I'm spending the night here in this chair."

"Shirley, I...I'd be grateful."

Carter heard and then witnessed Tom's love for Shirley from the glow in his eyes. Carter knew his mother would only have been happy to see Tom in love again. They'd loved each other so much. The memory of them together filled him like an inflating balloon. He swallowed, suppressing it.

"Then I'll leave you two for a few minutes." Carter gently pressed Tom's hand and waved good-bye. He walked farther down the corridor and stopped at the room number he'd been given for Audra. He'd last seen her in the frantic ER.

Now she was sitting in the chair beside her bed, still wearing her hospital gown and robe. The ugly shapeless gown didn't detract from her loveliness. But she looked downhearted and her hands were bandaged. He held out the bag of fresh clothing that Shirley had packed. "Hi." Then as he thought of Audra beating out the fire on Tom's shirt with her bare hands, his throat closed up on him.

She stood and accepted the bag, their fingertips touching. "I'll just be a moment." Her voice was low and rough from the smoke just like Tom's.

Carter kept contact with her a fraction of a second longer than he should have. Then he stepped back into the hallway to give her privacy. He heard the rings of the white curtain scraping as Audra pulled it around her. He tried not to think of

the woman so near and yet so beyond him. Why did circum-
stances keep drawing them together? Just so he'd notice how
her sunlit hair drifted around her shoulders in the lake breeze?
How her blue eyes lit up whenever her daughter smiled?

Soon Audra joined him. "Is Shirley with Tom?"

He tried to reel in his marked reaction to her, conceal any
evidence of it. "Yes."

"Is Evie with them?"

"No, Evie is spending the night with your mother and
sister."

Audra halted and stared up at him. "With my mother?"

Carter nodded. "Let's go." As he led her along to Tom's
room, he couldn't stop his gaze from drifting to her. When they
reached the room, she entered and hugged Shirley. Tom
reached out and took Audra's bandaged hand with obvious
care. She hesitated and then took a step forward.

"Audra, thank you," Tom said. "The doctor told me I'd
have been much worse off if you hadn't—"

Audra burst into tears and rushed from the room. Shirley
started to go after her and then halted. "Carter, please, will you
take care of Audra? Lois is going to pick me up here early in
the morning so we can help Audra with her morning baking.
Don't worry about me and Tom." When Carter delayed
following Audra, Shirley pushed him toward the door.

———

WITH HER HEAD BOWED and her hands tucked under her
arms, Audra waited just outside the door. Then Carter was
with her again, his masculine strength beckoning her.
"I'm...sorry for running off like that." She didn't look up,
hiding her teary eyes. She felt crumpled like dough without
enough leavening to rise. "It just brought it all back. I was so
frightened."

"No problem." He took her elbow. "Let's get out of here. Hospitals depress me."

The power underlying Carter's gentle grip heartened Audra. Suddenly she was able to inhale fully again. As the oxygen filled her lungs, she let him steer her out of the maze of hospital corridors and through the check-out procedure. Finally, he was helping her into his Jeep.

The summer evening was well advanced. A golden twilight was fading and ribbons of purple layered the darkening sky. The sky reflected her mood. Fluorescent gold weighed down by heavy purple with more darkness coming. *How am I going to be able to work in the morning?* Her aching hands longed to rest in Carter's.

He sat in the driver's seat and turned on the Jeep. The radio had been left on. The voice of the local radio announcer came on. "...fourth fire in Winfield. Local business owners and residents are worried about this string of unexplained arsons. Sheriff Carter Harding was unavailable for—" Carter switched it off.

Audra had only thought of the fires in a personal way, but the announcer must be speaking the truth. These fires could definitely hurt the tourist trade. But she didn't say anything about this. Carter's tight-lipped, rigid profile told her how he was feeling about the crimes. He was being held responsible for not putting an end to them. What if he couldn't find out who was doing this? And what if her new worry was true? Feeling helpless, she rested her hands in her lap and pursed her lips to keep back tears.

When they reached the highway out of town, he turned to her. "How are you feeling? Your hands?"

She leaned her head back on the headrest, trying not to imagine resting it on Carter's shoulder. "I'm sorry I gave way like that. It's just..." Maybe she shouldn't bring up the fires. But that's what was on both their minds, wasn't it?

"Just what?"

She let out a sigh, ready to voice her fear. "It occurred to me today that all the fires except for the first have affected someone close to me. It made me feel...responsible." She gathered up her courage. *Saying this out loud, Lord, is so difficult.* "Do you...do you think someone is really to...get to me through them?"

"No, I don't." His answer was swift and strong. "Wouldn't it be easier just to set your place on fire and be done with it?"

"Maybe the fire-setter wants to make me lose sleep first. Make me miserable."

"You might be correct," Carter said in a different voice, his official-sounding, give-nothing-away voice. "But who would have a grudge against you?"

Audra thought immediately of the irate after-hour phone calls. But why would *he* want to get back at her? Surely the shoe was on the other foot in this. In any case, bringing up the phone calls to Carter was impossible. Weakness swept over her. She felt herself folding up like a wildflower at dusk. "No one comes to mind," she muttered.

"Are you sure? You took a long time answering." Carter cast a suspicious glance her way.

"I'm sure," she replied, eyes forward. "But maybe I've upset someone without realizing it. So they enjoy worrying, plaguing me. Like a cat playing with a bird before it eats it."

"That happens in psychological thrillers," Carter replied with a shake of his head, "but in real life, we find that when we finally arrest the perpetrator, most crimes are pretty straightforward. Profit and revenge are the most common motives."

Audra sighed painfully. Her throat and lungs still caught and hitched a bit from inhaling smoke. She glanced at her watch. She had some minutes to wait before taking her next pain pill though her bandaged hands already throbbed. In the shadows, her unruly gaze shifted to the sheriff's profile again.

"I'm not surprised that you might begin to feel this is personal," Carter said. "The same idea crossed my mind. I mean, Tom is my stepdad."

"But the other fires don't have anything to do with you— not even the one at Shirley's." She dragged her eyes from Carter and looked down at her hands.

"It would be if the person responsible knows how close Tom and Shirley are."

Cars passed them, wheels whining. "Then that implicates most everyone in town."

Carter nodded gravely.

Being alone with this man distracted her. She told herself to concentrate on the fire, not on the sheriff. "Did you get any new evidence at Tom's?"

"Whoever did this rigged a trip wire at the back gate that set off a pretty powerful blast. The trip wire ignited a very short fuse connected to gasoline in a large metal gas drum Tom had in the shop. I found its remains scattered over the yard. The arsonist also filled and capped several more containers, some large, some small, with more gasoline and kerosene so that after the fire got started, there would be subsequent explosions—"

"Like the one that nearly knocked me out." And made her hands temporarily useless. How was she going to roll dough in a few hours?

"Yes. Anyway, our fire-setter is becoming more skilled and therefore, more dangerous. I keep wondering who would know all this stuff about incendiary explosives and fires. There doesn't seem to be anyone even remotely connected with the fires who would have a background in this kind of crime."

"Brent and I were talking about that just the other night. He said with easy access to the Internet, anybody could get this information." She shrugged. "Anybody with a computer could get all the instructions needed to set a booby trap."

Carter snorted. "Thank you very much, Information Highway."

"Who do you think did it?" Then she bit her lip. Should she have asked this of a sheriff? She'd forgotten for a moment that Carter was the sheriff—he'd become just Carter, her friend.

More than your friend? her conscience pointed out. She ignored it. This was too important. "Or can't you tell me who you suspect?"

Carter lifted one shoulder. "I know of one person who hates Tom—Doyle Keski."

She nodded, pursing her lips. "And...maybe I shouldn't discuss that with you, but Chad worries me..." Her voice faltered.

"Tom told me the night before last that he'd docked Chad's pay because he'd taken an afternoon off without permission."

She wrinkled her brow. "I don't think that would trigger something as drastic as blowing up Tom's shop, do you?"

"I don't know. With his history, Chad is TNT with a very short fuse just asking to be lit. I've seen it before with kids who've been subjected to violence. They are easily triggered and usually act out the violence they've suffered."

"Do you really think Chad would do it?" she objected, even though she was the one who brought up his name. "He likes working with Tom. And in spite of the resentful things he says, I think he likes being with Tom. I mean, Chad couldn't miss the stark difference between Doyle and Tom."

"That might have been what triggered this."

She questioned him with a glance.

"Chad isn't thinking very clearly. He's only fourteen, and his feelings about his dad are all mixed up. He might feel that setting these fires so ingeniously would impress his dad. And the trip wire was set at the back gate, not the back door where Tom broke the wire. He was still nearer the alley than the door.

If it had been triggered at the door, he could have been burned much, much worse than he was, or even killed."

Audra hadn't considered that. But it made sense. That someone had stopped short of causing more serious injury. The burden she'd carried lightened a bit. "I really care about Chad. He's been sweet to Evie and at first, so appreciative of Shirley taking him as her foster son."

"I think the reappearance of Doyle in town has ratcheted up Chad's anxiety. He loves and wants to be close to Doyle and at the same time, hates his dad and wants to be protected from him. That's a volatile mixture of strong emotions." Carter paused and then muttered, "And I should know."

Drawn nearer to him, Audra identified first the deep vein of sympathy in Carter's tone. She echoed it silently. It was common knowledge that when Carter was around Evie's age, his parents divorced and then his mom married Tom. When Carter was around Chad's age, his mom died of cancer. After the funeral, Carter tried to move in with his dad, who was another Doyle Keski, and was sent back to Tom. After that rejection, a rebellious Carter spent all of his high school years in trouble with teachers and the law.

Which accounted for the shame evident in his final words. She knew all about Carter's youthful rebellion from her uncle, who'd given a highly negative version, and from Shirley, who'd given a much kinder viewpoint. Should she say something? A silence yawned between them. "I don't believe my uncle when he talks about you and Sarah," she murmured at last.

"Thanks." His shadowed face—so determined, so compelling to her—twisted into a grimace. "But I was as wild then as your uncle says." Carter closed his lips. Summer night had finally come with its lingering glow on the horizon.

"Carter, I was only Evie's age then, and all I remember of Sarah was her shouting matches with her father." Audra wanted to add that her uncle was repeating the same grievous mistake with Brent, but didn't. "I'm sorry Sarah died so young, but I don't think you should carry guilt over your...wildness. When we're young, we all do things we regret." Like having a baby with a man who hadn't really loved her. And setting up her sweet little girl to be hurt by her father's rejection.

"I know I'd have ended up in prison or maybe like Sarah, dead before I saw thirty. I owe my life to Tom and how he demonstrated God's love toward me. You know that when I was seventeen, out of stupidity I nearly killed a kid in a fight at a party." He glanced in her direction.

She forced herself not to reach out to him, but she ached to comfort him.

"If I'd been a few months older," Carter said, "or if the judge hadn't listened to Tom's plea on my behalf, I'd have been tried as an adult. As it was, I served some time in a juvenile facility, went on probation, and after not getting into any further trouble, my record was expunged."

He dragged in air. "I owe everything to Tom, and I'm going to find out who hurt him like this. I'll bring whoever it is to justice." His final words promised unmistakable retribution.

Audra rested a bandaged hand on his arm, watching the headlights of another car flash over his face. His profile was a strong one with a firm jaw and chin. Carter had gone through the fiery furnace of rejection just as Chad had. Just as she had when her mother rejected her. He'd come through it a loving stepson and a better person with a reputation as a good friend.

The image of his lifting Evie into his arms flickered in her mind's eye. Her heart softened another degree. This man was becoming part of her life. Should she let the process continue? Carter wasn't the kind of man who led a woman on, and she'd not dated anyone since breaking up with Evie's father. Evie had to come first.

Frightened of this line of thought and all it might imply,

she dropped her hand and switched topics. "Why did my mother take Evie home?"

"She helped Shirley with your morning café trade."

"She what?" Audra sat bolt upright.

"Shirley took Evie to the café to see what she could do to salvage your risen dough and sell coffee." He shrugged. "When Megan arrived, she called your mom and told her about your injuries. And—"

"Mother called me at the hospital this afternoon," Audra interrupted. "She wanted to know how badly I was hurt and if I had health insurance."

"Shirley told me Lois showed up at your café and made and served coffee and tea while Shirley made sweet rolls."

Audra's own helplessness corroded her mood further. *Lord, I need to be able to work with my hands.* "Shirley shouldn't have. I owe her so much already." Again, shaming, undeniable tears began spilling from her eyes. Her emotions were all over the place. Now she understood what the doctor had said about an emotional reaction to the fire. That she might experience exactly what she was feeling now.

Carter slowed and pulled off the road at a public wayside. He parked in the deserted well-tended clearing with a picnic shelter and brick outdoor facilities amidst the dense forest. From the shadows, a white-tailed deer darted away into the evergreens.

"Hey, Audra, come on. Everything's okay. Tom will be out of the hospital in a few days. You're going to be all right." He stroked her back, making her pulse race through her veins. And at the same time calming her.

Her sense of being out of control ebbed. She breathed in fresh air from the open window and made herself settle. "I'm okay. It's still the shock of seeing the flames." She didn't want to go over again what had happened this morning. Her hands were throbbing in earnest now. "Do you have any water? I need to take a pain pill." She looked down at her bandaged hands, wondering how she was going to knead and shape dough in the morning.

Carter rummaged in the backseat and brought out a cup. "I'll go work the pump—"

"No—"

"It'll just take me a minute." He opened his door and strode to the shelter where a glossy dark green picnic table had been placed near a bright red old-fashioned hand pump.

Audra got out and hurried after him. She took the mug from him while he pumped the handle. Cold water poured out of the pump, splashing her sandaled feet. She started to put the mug under the flow when Carter took it from her. "We don't want your bandages to get wet."

Suddenly weak and so tired, she moved backward and collapsed onto the bench of the picnic table. She took the mug and swallowed her pill. The water was icy and soothed her raw throat. "Thanks."

He sat down beside her and she welcomed the protective arm he put around her. "Are you in a lot of pain?"

She shook her head. "No, just enough," she said, trying to smile. Embarrassing tears still threatened. She shut her eyes tightly and looked away from him, but the tears leaked out anyway.

He pulled her closer to him and she didn't have the strength to resist. She turned to him and began to weep onto his chest.

"Let it out," he murmured, tenderly stroking her back. "You've been through an awful experience. You can't just ignore it. You've been injured physically and shocked by violence. Let it out. You'll feel better."

The tears turned into several minutes of sobbing. Finally, she gasped for air and began wiping her face with her fingertips. "I'm so—"

His forefinger lifted her chin and then he was kissing her. She leaned into him. Her arms crept around his neck. Finally, he ended the kiss and she lowered her arms, pulling away.

"I'm sorry—" he began.

Please don't apologize. I wanted you to kiss me. She couldn't deny this, but it sent shivers of panic through her. She reached up and pressed her fingers against his lips, stopping him. She didn't want to spoil the moment by discussing all the reasons why they shouldn't be sitting here on a public highway at a state wayside kissing. She rested her head against his arm.

Audra voiced her main worry. "I don't know how I'm going to do my baking in the morning. I can't afford to stay closed for the week to ten days that the doctor said my hands would take to heal."

"Shirley said Lois is picking her up in the morning and they're coming to help you open."

"I just don't understand..." She fell silent, not wanting to discuss her strained relationship with her mother.

"I think you're going to have to accept their help."

"You're probably right." Maybe with Shirley's help she could manage to keep the coffee and tea part of her business going. But she'd lose trade. People wanted more than just coffee. Suddenly exhausted, she drooped against him.

He wrapped his arm around her again. "I need to get you home." He drew her up and they got back onto the quiet highway and drove on. His headlights on the pavement were mesmerizing, but his comforting presence was powerful in the silent vehicle.

"You didn't get any useful clues, then?" Audra leaned back against the seat, distancing herself from him.

"Nothing. Not a fingerprint. No one saw anyone lurking around. None of the materials used to set the fire have any distinctive identity to trace. None of them would be difficult to get. In fact, most of the booby trap was made up of materials from Tom's shop."

"Is there any chance that these fires aren't connected?"

Carter made a dismissive sound. "I've been keeping back the one clue that connects each of these fires. And when I tell you, you won't believe me."

"Why? What's the clue?" She turned toward him.

"This is in strictest confidence," he said, giving her a stern glance.

"Of course."

"Pennies."

"Pennies?" She looked at him, suddenly wide-eyed.

"The arsonist always leaves a stack of pennies at each crime scene."

"Why pennies?"

"If I could figure that out, I'd probably know who's setting fires and leaving behind handfuls of pennies."

Audra rubbed her taut forehead. "This is too much for me. I thought my biggest challenges this summer would be keeping up with my heavy schedule of early and late hours—not this."

He touched her arm and then pulled back. "You'll feel better in the morning."

She doubted it but didn't want to say so. She closed her eyes and concentrated on the whir of the tires on the pavement, not her responsiveness to the strong man beside her. With Carter so near, her fears gradually subsided. What was she going to do with her growing feelings for him? They appeared to be next to impossible to dismiss.

———

EARLY THE NEXT MORNING AUDRA walked through Shirley's empty house. Her mind buzzed. How was she going to work dough? And where was Chad?

At four o'clock, when the squawking alarm had awakened her, she'd wished she had a sledgehammer handy to smash it. She'd sat up stiffly in bed and realized she'd slept in one position all night like a mummy—too exhausted to even roll over in her sleep. She'd moved slower getting ready, too. Her bandaged hands throbbed, making her fumble with her buttons and zipper.

On her way downstairs, she'd knocked on Chad's door and there'd been no answer. She'd cautiously opened the door and found his bed empty. Where had he gone off to at this hour? Should she call Carter?

She'd tell Shirley as soon as she got to work. Even if she couldn't figure out how, with her hands still bandaged and hurting—she would do her work. She couldn't afford to lose any more business. She patted the slacks pocket where her pain pills rattled in their plastic bottle. Her footsteps echoed through the sleeping house as she exited through the front hall instead of the kitchen. She couldn't face walking down the alley where she'd experienced the fire yesterday morning. And on top of everything else, where was Chad?

Dawn brightened the lingering gray of night, promising another good day for business. But all the way through the sleepy town to her Victorian, she fretted. She let herself inside the front gate and through the front door. She heard voices. And stilled with fear. Intruders?

Then she recognized the voices. Shirley and Chad? She hurried through the house to the large professional kitchen in the rear. Shirley and Chad stood side by side at the counter where Shirley was demonstrating how to roll out dough after its first rise.

Audra halted in the doorway, gawking at them.

"Morning, Audra." Her mother's voice called her attention to the other workstation where she was filling sweet roll dough with raspberry jam.

"What...? I...you," Audra stammered.

"We're here to help," her mother explained. "How are you, dear?" She came over and looked Audra up and down. Then she leaned over and kissed Audra's cheek. "I would have come to the hospital, but Evie needed both me and Megan to keep her spirits up. And I didn't think visiting you and Tom at the hospital would be best for her. I hope you agree."

"Yes. Yes. But..." Audra couldn't remember the last time her mother had kissed her, and she couldn't take in all the unexpected help.

"You didn't think you could work dough with those hands, did you?" Her mother arched one eyebrow.

Audra felt as if she were chasing a paper blown by the wind. "I...was going to try."

"Foolishness." Her mother shook her head decidedly and turned back to her workstation.

"Audra," Shirley informed her, "I'm teaching Chad how to work dough into different shapes. He'll need a new summer job now that Tom's place must be rebuilt."

"But I can't afford—"

"I'll be paying Chad," her mother said. "And I don't want to hear a word about it. I'm your mother, and you're working yourself much too hard."

Audra's mouth opened and closed a few times. When she finally tried to object, her mother raised the thin spatula she was using and made a sharp gesture which obviously signified, No discussion!

Nonplussed, Audra plumped down on one of the work stools. "Thank you. I really appreciate this."

"I recorded a message last night explaining about the fire and your injuries," Shirley said. "That will take care of your pizza customers. And before Carter drove me to the hospital yesterday, Brent helped me measure the ingredients for this morning's dough and set the timers."

"And I picked her up this morning from the hospital and Chad met us here," Audra's mother finished, efficiently filling a sheet pan with rolls and sliding them into the nearby oven. "We told him not to wake you. We hoped you'd have enough sense to sleep in. Megan will be here around seven o'clock with Evie to work the morning shift as usual."

Audra managed a rueful smile. "I see that I'm easily replaced. Chad, thanks for helping out."

Chad cast her a dark glance. "Don't you think I set the fire at Tom's like everyone else?"

Behind the anger, Audra heard the pain in the teen's voice. "No, Chad, I don't."

"Neither do I," her mother said. "You and Tom seemed to get along well together."

Chad looked surprised at this unexpected vote of confidence. But his face hardened. "Don't you think I set your shed on fire?" he demanded.

"No. I did ask the sheriff if you might have been smoking and dropped a butt into some dry grass. That's the kind of thing teenagers do to give their parents prematurely gray hair. But he said it had been set with a fuse." Audra's mother looked at Chad. "Why would you set my shed on fire? You don't even know me."

"I used to set fires," Chad confessed, bowing his head lower over the dough he was shaping into rounds for sweet rolls.

"Well, I'm sure that was before you came to live with Shirley and Tom," her mother replied. "You'll find as you get older we all do things which later we wish we could undo." The words carried some special weight. Was her mother saying something personal?

In the momentary silence after this, Shirley spoke up then, instructing and encouraging Chad. Audra stood up. "Well, at least I can take the baked goods out of the ovens." She put on her apron and oven mitts. The four of them worked with a few mistakes and much laughter and then Megan and Evie arrived.

Evie ran to Audra and then halted, pointing to Audra's bandaged hands. "Mama, your hands are hurt."

"I'll be all right, baby." Audra bent down and hugged her. "The bandages will come off soon."

Evie hugged her back. "The sheriff told me yesterday that he'll take me to go see Tom today. Is Tom hurt bad?"

Audra brushed back her daughter's dark silken hair. "Tom will be all right and you shouldn't be bothering the sheriff."

"He likes it when I talk to him. And I asked him if he would take us to the fireworks on Fourth of July, too."

"Evie! No." Audra's face warmed. Embarrassment swelled inside her. "You shouldn't have asked him that."

Evie ignored this. "The sheriff said yes, if it was okay with you, and that I should ask you. But Mama, I want him to go with us. I want him to pick me up and put me on his shoulders. Cassie always sits on her daddy's shoulders to watch the fireworks. But I don't got a daddy so I asked the sheriff."

I don't got a daddy. The words slashed Audra's heart in two. She nearly rubbed the spot over her heart to staunch the pain. Silence blossomed and grew in the kitchen. "I'll be working that night, baby."

Evie propped her hands on her hips. "Mama, I'm not a baby—"

Audra held up a hand. "I'm sorry. I'm sorry. You're not a baby anymore."

Megan swung Evie up into her arms and jiggled her playfully. "Come on, Miss I'm-not-a-baby-anymore, we have to get our aprons on and make sure everything is set up for your mom." The two slipped on their aprons and Megan tied both of them. Then she paused on their way to the front and said, "Audra, I'll work the pizza shift on the Fourth of July. Evie deserves her big night out on the sheriff's shoulders."

"Megan!" Audra exclaimed, feeling her pride come undone. How could she look Carter in the face?

Megan laughed and swept Evie away with her.

Audra turned and found her mother smiling. "My granddaughter certainly knows what she wants and how to get it."

Shirley chuckled. "And we all know she wants a daddy."

Face still on fire, Audra didn't trust herself to speak. The combination of hurt and humiliation throbbed like her injured hands. She'd tell Sheriff Harding that he could come up with a good excuse for not taking her and Evie to the carnival. Everyone in town would see them. It would spark more talk than their sitting in church together. And worse yet, if her uncle were there, he might even cause a scene.

But her daughter's words, "I don't got a daddy," continued to bee-sting her heart. How could she make Evie realize that this wasn't the time for love...for her? She was just too busy this summer. And she still couldn't believe a man would want her with a child. Being kind to a friend's daughter was very different from assuming responsibility for that child. And she and Evie were a package deal.

Still, the memory of Carter's kiss the night before taunted Audra. *I do have feelings for him but I'm not going to act on them, so that means I'm leading him on. I have to make up my mind, break it off, and stick to that. I can't keep giving in to the touch of his hands and the way he smiles at Evie.*

But she knew her resolutions had no foundation. She'd worked hard to be independent. Letting Carter into her life... Could she take that chance?

Chapter 8

On the evening of the Fourth, Evie clung excitedly to Carter's hand as they moved among the fun-seeking crowd. Residents, summer people, and tourists packed the street along the end of the wharf and marina. In front of them the blue water of Lake Superior glistened in the sun. Behind them across the street were the many shops and then the rise up from the lake. At the end of the carnival booths, the street rose gently toward another street and alley. The carnival rides had been set up there in the larger open area. But of course, nowhere was really open with this large crowd milling around.

The long summer day lingered with unusual heat and humidity. Carter had been surprised when Evie had invited him, and he'd see to it that she had a good time tonight. But Audra walked beside him, looking tense. *Is she worried about gossip? Maybe her uncle seeing us together?*

Carter wasn't officially on duty, but he wore his short-sleeved khaki uniform shirt and brown trousers he'd worked in all day and was always unofficially on duty—especially on the Fourth of July and other large gatherings. Audra and Evie wore matching outfits, sharp-looking short-sleeved white blouses with blue stars, red shorts, and sandals.

Audra's nearness enticed him. Beyond her graceful and easy sway, everything drew his notice—her small waist, her translucent skin. As they edged toward the merry-go-round, he tried to steer "his" two ladies away from neighbors. But the whole of Winfield appeared to be on hand and seemed delighted and intrigued to see the three of them together.

Off to his left, Carter glimpsed Florence approaching them. He braced himself for whatever might come out of her mouth.

"Well, well," Florence commented, smirking at them.

"Hi, Mrs. LeVesque." Evie greeted their unpredictable neighbor who wore one of her late husband's threadbare shirts, trousers, and an old fishing hat with lures. "The sheriff bringed us."

"I see," Florence said, giving both him and Audra a very obvious once-over. "Are you three having a good time?"

Evie did a little jig. "I'm going to ride the merry-go-round and it's going to go real fast round and round. And the sheriff's going to win me a prize, too."

"Evie, I said I'd try," Carter cautioned.

Florence's smirky smile broadened. "Don't listen to him, Evie. A girl can never tell what might happen to her when she's out with a handsome man." She winked at Audra and then strolled away.

Carter glanced at Audra. She pursed her lips. Then she looked up, her smile bright and full. "Here we are, the line for the merry-go-round."

He had no idea what had caused her smile. But he smiled back at her and led them to the line of parents with their bouncing, chattering offspring.

Though he made himself focus on Evie, Audra affected him. Snatches of old love songs played in his mind. Still, he noted that Audra's chin rose a fraction every time someone glanced curiously in their direction. What did that mean?

Finally, their turn came to hand in their bright turquoise-blue tickets. Carter lifted Evie up and swung her onto the merry-go-round. She'd already pointed out the horse she wanted, the one that had pink ribbons painted into its mane. Carter set her astride it.

Evie clutched the pole and squealed greetings to her friend Cassie who had taken the horse right in front of her. "Cassie, look! The sheriff bringed me and my mama!"

Carter smiled ruefully at Audra.

Grinning, Cassie and her parents waved back at them. Audra appeared to be putting on a good act of not noticing everyone noticing them together. The distinctive merry-go-round music began and the ride jerked to a start. Carter stood on the inside of the ride at Evie's side and Audra stood on the other. To keep balance on the moving platform, both of them loosely held on to the rising and lowering pole with one hand and rested the other hand on the rump of the fancy wooden horse.

Over Audra's head, Carter watched the collage of faces twirl by and then he glanced down at his hand lying so close to Audra's. Her hand still bore marks of her brave act of putting out the fire that had charred Tom's shirt and blistered his chest. For one brief second, Carter felt the urge to lift her hand to his lips, to pay tribute to its reddened and roughened skin.

No. Not here. Not now. That gesture would give everyone in town grist to gossip about for weeks, if not months. He tried to ignore the way her hand continued to beckon him. But slowly he moved his hand and then he couldn't help himself, he covered hers with his. Would she pull away?

Audra's eyes flashed up to meet his. What did they tell him? He couldn't decipher the message there. But she didn't pull her hand away. Separated only by inches, he let himself study her, noting every tiny freckle on her clear gold-tinged complexion. His longing to be near her expanded within and he found it hard to swallow. *I want to kiss you again, Audra.*

The ride ended, jolting him back to reality. Reluctantly his hand broke contact with Audra's. He lifted Evie off the ride. He bent to put her down on the ground, but she clung to his neck.

"Hold my hand," she pleaded, her eyes drifting to Cassie.

Carter followed her gaze and saw that Cassie's dad was holding his little girl's hand. "Sure." Carter straightened up with Evie at his side. Audra strolled beside him. She gave him a mysterious smile and then rested her hand on his arm.

Her touch hit him, blinding him with sudden light, a lift. It was as if he'd been in a dark room and someone swept open the curtains. Joy, bright joy, radiated inside him. Audra must feel the need to touch him, too. He couldn't keep from grinning. The three of them being here together felt suddenly so right.

Then, from the end of the block came shouting, people hurrying toward the sheriff. "Fight! Fight!" echoed over the crowd. His exultant mood shattered. Carter turned to Audra and shifted Evie to her. "Stay back!"

He began shoving forward, going against the flow, elbowing his way through the surge of people fleeing toward safety. Then he saw the two combatants, Brent and Chad. He made a sound of disgust and pushed through the remaining crowd around the two. "Stop!" he shouted. "Stop that! No fighting in public!"

The two teens ignored Carter. Chad threw a punch, but his own momentum took him off balance and he fell on top of Brent. The two began thrashing around on the ground, grunting and cursing each other. Carter reached down and grabbed the backs of both their collars and hauled them to their feet. Both tried to wrench themselves out of his grip.

Neither succeeded but the effort caused Chad to sway alarmingly. Carter held on tightly.

Chad turned toward him, yelling insults at him. The liquor on his breath blasted Carter's nostrils. So that's what's started this. Whiskey courage. He shook Chad. "Where'd you get it?"

"Get what?" Chad slurred.

"The booze." He shook Chad again. "Tell me!"

"Take your hands off my son!" Hal Ramsdel's voice boomed over the circle of onlookers.

Great, just what he needed. Carter swung to face him.

Ramsdel burst through the bystanders and grabbed at Carter's shirt. "Let go of my son!"

"Uncle Hal, please!" Audra pleaded, Evie under her arm. "Stay out of this."

Carter shook Ramsdel off. "These two were fighting in public! This has nothing to do with you!"

"That's right, old man!" Brent jeered in agreement. "I don't need you protecting me!" Brent lunged toward Chad, his hands clawing for Chad's throat.

Breathing hard, Carter kept his arms extended like a clothesline pole, separating the two teens. Both struggled to free themselves and attack each other again.

Ramsdel, red in the face, tried to yank Brent from Carter's hold. It became a three-way tug-of-war with Carter, the linchpin, trying to stay on his feet. Sweat trickled down both sides of Carter's face. How much longer could he keep this up?

"Stop!" Carter roared at last, stunning the two teens into obedience. But Ramsdel snatched at his son one more time. Brent resisted and tossed a vulgar insult at his father. Hal raised his fist to his son.

Then before Carter's eyes, it all happened in slow motion. Evie bolted out of the crowd, launching herself at her great-uncle, Audra at her heels. "Stop!" her shrill little voice shrieked. "Don't you hurt Brent! Don't you hurt my cousin!"

Her voice stunned them all. They froze, staring at her.

Brent recovered himself first. "Evie, I'll be all right." He took her hand. "I can take care of myself."

"You got blood on your face." She began to whimper. "Why do you got to fight with Chad?" Through her tears, she nailed Chad, too, with a pleading look. "Why do you got to hurt my cousin?"

For a moment, Carter hoped Evie had defused the situation. Audra bent to draw Evie away.

But Hal tried to charge Carter. He lost his balance, stumbled, and fell. When he hit the ground, he was looking up at Carter. A deluge of insults and vulgarity poured out of his mouth.

Carter let Brent go. Brent dropped to his knees and folded Evie into his arms, his hand over her ears as if trying to shield her from the unstaunched flow of insults. Audra stared, openmouthed at her uncle.

Red flickered in front of Carter's vision. Over the roaring in his ears, he heard Brent's voice, "Stop that! Shut up, you stupid old man! Shut—up!"

Carter dragged in some fresh air. Chad had stopped struggling and stood swaying. Carter let go of him, leaned over, and stroked Evie's fine soft hair. "It will be all right, little one. Hush." Audra huddled with her arms around both Evie and Brent.

Ramsdel struggled to his feet. "This is all your fault!" he shouted at Carter.

Carter didn't know what he meant and didn't care. "Brent," he said, fighting to sound calm, "get up. I need to talk to you and Chad about this incident. Come on." He swiped his hand over his perspiring forehead.

"My son doesn't have to go anywhere with you!" Ramsdel shouted.

Carter ignored him and motioned Brent over. "Everyone,

move on!" Carter ordered the onlookers. "Show's over! Move on!"

Ramsdel shouted, "How anyone could have thought that a reprobate like you should be sheriff is beyond me!"

Most people edged away from the unpleasant scene. Carter motioned for Brent and Chad to follow him. Leaning closer to Audra, he said, sounding rough to his own ears, "Go buy Evie some kettle corn and I'll meet you by——"

"And you!" Ramsdel turned to verbally attack Audra. "I thought you were smarter than this. How can you let this man, this murderer, touch you?"

"Stop saying bad things," Evie fired back. "You're being mean!"

Audra stepped between her uncle and daughter. "Uncle Hal, I think you should calm down." Her voice was low but firm. "This can't be good for you——"

Ramsdel shouted an insult at her.

Red exploded in front of Carter's eyes. Ramsdel turned and was stalking away, still tossing back threats: "This isn't the last of this! I'll make you rue the day you were born!"

Did he mean Audra or Carter? Rage shuddered through Carter in hot waves. He forced himself to breathe normally. Brent was still hugging Evie protectively. Chad had slipped away and vanished into the crowd.

Brent straightened up. "Chad started it."

Carter nodded, the rage evaporating, leaving him suddenly hollow with guilt about his own display of fury. *Lord, why do I still get so angry? I know it's not what You wish. Why did Ramsdel have to come back to town? I was fine until he popped up again.* But wasn't he just attempting to shift responsibility for his anger onto Ramsdel? Guilt over making excuses chafed Carter's conscience. He was ashamed to look into Audra's eyes. Carter lifted his cell phone from his pocket and alerted dispatch to have all on-duty deputies look for Chad and bring him in for his own protection.

Facing Brent, he detected no alcohol on him, so he might be telling the truth. "Don't let me catch you fighting in a public place again, got it?" Carter spoke sharply. Angry at himself and Brent, he had trouble looking at Audra. He took refuge in confronting Brent. "Audra told me you were working with Megan this evening at Audra's Place."

Brent bristled visibly. "We shut down at eight o'clock. The phone stopped ringing way before then so we closed up tight and left."

"You still got blood on your face," Evie said, sounding concerned.

"Let's go to my place—" Audra began.

"No, Audra," Brent objected, his voice softening. "Don't let this spoil Evie's big Fourth of July date with the sheriff. I'll go clean up at the public restroom."

Shirley appeared with Tom at her side.

"Shirley," Carter said, "I don't want you to go looking for Chad. My deputies will be on the watch for him and bring him home."

Shirley frowned, but said, "Brent, come with us. It's quiet at my place." Her obvious concern for the teen showed plainly in her tone.

"Thanks, but I don't let him bother me." Brent looked up at the sheriff resentfully.

Carter wished he could say the same of Ramsdel. He recalled Audra's suspicion that her uncle might be close to a breakdown, and it now seemed more plausible—and more worrisome. Ramsdel had sounded out of control, beyond reason.

"Brent, come with us," Tom said. "We'll get you cleaned up and then you can go home or stay and watch the fireworks with us. Shirley and I are going to view the fireworks from her second-story landing. Come on."

"No, I'm going home," Brent declared and turned away.

Not meeting Audra's eyes, Carter squatted down in front of Evie. "Are you two okay?"

"I'm okay now," Evie said, fiercely hugging Carter's neck.

"Let's go to my place." Audra touched his arm lightly. "I need some quiet." Her voice quavered. "But are you...do you need to stay here, keep an eye on things?"

Even as he looked around and saw his deputies in the crowd handling the crowd, her hesitant touch grieved him. Being with him had made her a target for her uncle. "I'm not on duty. Maybe we should just go to Shirley's, too."

"No!" Evie objected. "No, you promised."

He looked to Audra for direction.

"Evie, we'll come right back." Audra took his elbow and led them away to the front of her café. "Promise."

As he walked beside her, her touch soothed his frayed nerves like a warm cream.

Audra unlocked the gate and led them into the Victorian house. "I'm sorry," she apologized. "Nothing is finished except for the kitchen and foyer. I'm planning on getting the upstairs done before Christmas. But for now, there are some lawn chairs in the parlor." She grinned suddenly. "My decorator likes the outdoorsy-resort look."

Trying to go along with her attempt to lighten the mood, Carter nodded and followed her through pocket doors into the bare room whose high ceiling and walls needed painting and hardwood floor needed refinishing. Audra invited him with a wave of her hand to sit in one of the striped cloth lawn chairs. He breathed in the scents redolent in the café, the whisper of coffee and cinnamon. But he was more aware of Audra than anything else in the house. She brightened even this bare room.

Evie slid her hand from his. "Mama, can I play on the porch?"

"Yes, but don't leave the porch."

"I won't." Evie ran out of the room. They were alone. Carter had to fold his hands to keep from reaching for Audra.

"There's a porch swing out there that she likes to lie in," Audra explained.

He nodded, still holding himself back. He found himself staring at her lips. The lower one was a bit fuller than the upper lip. Should he bring up what had just happened with her uncle? What was Audra thinking and feeling?

———

AUDRA LOOKED INTO CARTER'S eyes. She didn't want to let on how she still shook inside because of her uncle's out of control behavior. She remembered her mother's recent caution, "Please be careful, Audra. The sheriff seems like a good man, but you have Evie to consider." *As if I didn't know that. As if I haven't put Evie first since I left college expecting her and came to Winfield.*

Had her mother forgotten that she was the one who'd wanted Audra to go away to a maternity home, have Evie, and give her up for adoption? Audra's irritation mounted.

Suddenly, the desire to throw herself into Carter's protective arms rocked her. Instead she made herself sit down and rest her elbows on her knees, hiding her face in both hands. She tried to think of some topic to discuss, something that would conceal her reaction to Carter. She didn't want to think or talk about her uncle or her mother or Brent or the fires. She glanced up at Carter and then away. She spoke the first sentence that came to mind. "Where do you think Chad got the liquor?"

Carter shrugged. "I wouldn't put it past his dad to give him a bottle. He'll try anything to get Chad back in some way."

"Why?" she asked, remembering how firm Carter's chest had been when he'd held her that evening at the wayside. She'd felt so protected. "Doyle obviously doesn't love Chad."

Carter's mouth flattened. "I think it's more about Doyle's pride. Chad's his kid, you see."

She tried to focus on his words, but it was the sound of his voice that hushed over her like a soft lake breeze. The nape of her neck tingled. Here, alone with Carter, her defenses were melting. Trying to hold his effect on her at bay, she let slip out, "My uncle...I told you—he troubles me."

"He's beginning to get to me."

"But he couldn't be setting the fires." She covered her eyes, concealing how near she was to reaching for Carter. "I mean, what would he have against Tom?"

"Tom's my stepfather."

She inhaled sharply. "I know. But..." She rose abruptly. Restlessness wouldn't let her sit here any longer. If they didn't leave now, she'd embarrass both of them by throwing herself at Carter. "Let's not ruin Evie's special night. Let's go back and take her through the different games and buy her some cotton candy."

Unable to stop herself, she held her hand out to him. Rising, he took it. His touch set her heartbeat on high speed. Her lips tingled, recalling his kiss. Would he kiss her tonight? *I shouldn't want to kiss him.* But she'd never wanted another man's kiss as much she wanted Carter's.

———

THE TIME FOR THE TOWN'S fireworks display, always held at the waterfront, neared. Audra and Carter stood with Evie, who was waiting for the moment that he'd take her up on his shoulders to see the fireworks. Evie greeted everyone she saw and pointed out that she was with the sheriff—drawing even more attention to the threesome they made.

Audra recognized the speculation in the eyes of friends and neighbors. Well, let them wonder. Nothing would stop her from letting Carter make Evie happy. The stubborn summer sun, a bright bronze circle, finally slid below the horizon. Then over tranquil dark blue Lake Superior, the fireworks exploded to "Ahhhs" and then the next display brought "Ohhhhs." But more than the fireworks, her daughter's excitement fascinated Audra. Evie's innocent enjoyment of being lifted on Carter's shoulders to view the shimmering bursts of color and manmade thunder touched her mother-heart.

Finally, the grand finale burst above them. Crimson, sapphire, molten gold, and emerald, shimmering, glittering, dazzling, sparkling, flashing, flickering—shooting upward, outward, expanding, disintegrating again and again. And over all the crescendo of BOOMS.

Suddenly there was silence followed by raucous applause, shouts of pleasure, and whistles from the audience. Audra grinned and turned to watch Carter lift Evie down. Holding her around the waist, he swung her up and down. "How was that, munchkin?" he asked.

On the upward swing, Evie threw her arms around the sheriff's neck. "Wow!" she exclaimed, giggling. Looking around, she begged, "Piggyback me just a little longer. Please. Take me over there where the games are. Please."

Obligingly Carter swung her back up onto his broad shoulders. "You want to go through the games. Okay!" He headed toward the narrow aisle of games, ones like trying to knock down wooden pins with softballs. The tight aisle followed the lakefront. The evening breeze tried to penetrate the crowd, but they were packed together.

Walking beside Carter through the peopled lane, Audra

thought her heart would burst with happiness over Evie's triumphant smile. Why shouldn't she and Carter be together? *This is now, not twenty years ago. I'm not the little girl I was when Carter and Sarah dated. And Carter isn't the wild kid he was then. We've both changed, matured, and drawn closer to God. The old has passed away and the new has come.*

But how could her uncle understand letting God come in and change one's heart? After two wrecked marriages, he was blundering around and mishandling Brent without a clue.

Momentarily breathless in the mass of people all talking, laughing, squealing, Audra heard firecrackers hiss and crackle nearby. She looked around in the crush, trying to see who was throwing them. Apprehension flickered inside her.

"Who's setting off firecrackers in the middle of all these people?" Carter said into her ear.

More firecrackers erupted. Audra pressed more tightly to Carter and Evie, memories of the fire at Tom's sparking her fear.

"Fire!" a man shouted. Women shrieked. The crowd began to push forward.

Flames began licking up one of the game booths, setting the stuffed animal prizes alight. The lake breeze carried the flames across to the canvas to the food tent on the opposite side of them. Fire began devouring the khaki canvas. The night scene was suddenly bright with flames. Surrounding them on both sides of the midway.

Shouts of "Fire! Fire!" echoed over the hurrying crowd. In Audra, panic burst to life.

Someone shoved Audra from behind. She fought to keep her footing. Another booth caught fire and another. Flames leaped overhead. Shrieks filled her ears. Terror arced inside her. In a blink, the crowd surged into a mob.

Sparks fluttered down. Flaming canvas fragments. Pinprick burns. Audra felt herself being parted from Carter and Evie.

She grabbed for his arm. But the crowd surged behind her. Carrying her away. She struggled to stay on her feet. She shouted, "Carter! Evie!" Chaos swallowed the sound of her voice. The siren calling the volunteer firefighters wailed in the distance.

Booths on both sides of her blazed. Flames spreading. Frantic people pushed, shoved. All trying to get to the end of the midway and out. Flashes of memory—beating out Tom's shirt bright with fire—stoked her own panic. Terrified, she felt herself calling, screaming, "Carter! Evie!" But the crowd, shouting, "Fire! Fire!" overwhelmed her. The crowd carried Audra out of the narrow midway.

People crashed into the flimsy metal rail around the merry-go-round, climbed over the wreckage, swarming around the ride and into the widening street beyond. Landing on the merry-go-round, she clung to a pony pole like claiming a ship's mast in a storm. The pony became her shield. The metal roof too. She gasped for breath. Memory gripped her—her hands burned again as if afire.

Clutching the pole, Audra screamed, "Evie!" She imagined terrible scenes where the crowd knocked Evie from Carter's shoulders. Trampling her little girl. Audra's fear leaped higher and higher. She fought her own hysteria. *God, God, protect her; help me keep control.* She shuddered and braced herself against the chaos, swallowing her screams.

Then another siren roared above the chaos. And gunfire— two commanding bangs—and then a bullhorn, "Do not panic! Firefighters are on their way! Move out of the thoroughfare so the fire engine can reach the scene."

Carter's calm authoritative voice seemed to breach the madness. The screaming quieted. People still hurried but they looked around themselves as if awakening. Carter's strong voice over the bullhorn continued to give orders.

Still holding her place, Audra looked around, trying to

locate Evie. The fire engine sirens wailed, sounding closer. People moved, making way for the firefighters. Audra let them go, clung to the pole, trying to see Carter, Evie. She breathed prayer upon prayer.

The crowd stopped on the rise beyond the wharf to watch the blaze. The flames still roared behind Audra. Ash floated above and smoke streamed into the night sky. Frozen in place, Audra sheltered under the canopy over the carousel. The fire engine arrived. As the firefighters hooked hoses to hydrants and began battling the blaze, Audra watched them beat back the fire. *Evie. Carter. Please, Lord.*

Carter was suddenly beside her. From the haven of his arms, Evie was reaching out to Audra. "Mama! Mama! The sheriff 'tected me. Mama!"

Audra opened her arms, not just to Evie but to Carter, and the two of them embraced—Audra and Carter sheltering Evie between them. This night had put into reality her deepest fear, the recurring nightmare of not being able to protect Evie. Audra dragged in air to hold off tears. She rubbed her face against Carter's shirt, drawing in his scent. With the last bit of her self-control, she stopped herself from lifting her mouth to his.

"You were smart to stay still and grab hold of something stronger than the crowd," Carter said. He stepped back. He looked around at the firefighters about a third of a block away. "I think you'll be safe here for a while. I need to talk to the fire chief and then I'll walk you home. Okay?" But he didn't wait for her assent. He hurried toward the blaze that the firefighters were already getting under control.

Her knees weak with relief and aftershock, Audra sank onto one of the merry-go-round benches and settled Evie on her lap. Evie clung to her. "I was scared," she whimpered.

"The sheriff had you. You were safe with him." Audra held on to the memory of his touch just moments before. And then she admitted it. Carter Harding had become the most dangerous man in Winfield—the most dangerous to her heart.

———

LATER, WITH EVIE ASLEEP against his shoulder and her thin legs dangling down his chest, Carter paused outside Shirley's back door and turned to Audra. The emotional turmoil had drained her, making her even more vulnerable to him. She tried to think of something to say besides "Hold me." She cleared her throat. "Where did you get the bullhorn?"

"I left my Jeep behind the Anchor Inn. I ran with Evie, put her inside, loaded my rifle with blanks and shot into the air. There's nothing like a rifle firing to get people's attention."

Stars glowed overhead. She tried to focus on them and not him. "You expected trouble, then?"

"No, if I'd expected trouble, I wouldn't have taken you and Evie." His voice softened. "I wouldn't want anything to happen to you two." He turned slightly, his voice businesslike. "I just think it's good to always be prepared for the worst."

Audra fell silent. Was he fighting the same impulse? Did he want to hold her, too? Of their own accord her eyes lifted to his. Voices sounded in the distance. Shirley's house was quiet. The undeniable pull toward him tugged Audra. She reached for the doorknob behind her, still resisting temptation, still taking refuge in words. "Who do you think tossed the firecrackers? And did they do it to start the fire?"

"No way of knowing yet." His deep voice was soft around the edges as if he were speaking words of love to her.

His voice, so rich and deep, somehow sensitized the skin at her nape. "Maybe just kids?" she suggested, desperately clinging to their conversation.

He shrugged. Evie snuffled softly in her sleep. He grinned at this and gently patted her back.

This gesture, at last, compelled Audra forward. She laid a hand on his cheek. *Please, Carter, kiss me.* As if anticipating the touch of his lips, her lips tingled. She leaned her mouth toward his.

He whispered her name. Then slanted his head and moved it forward.

She held her breath, counting off the seconds as his lips drew nearer.

"Mama." Shifting in his arms, Evie woke up and rubbed her eyes. "Are we home yet?"

"Yes, Evie." Feeling a sharp claw of disappointment, Audra helped her daughter down from Carter's arms. "Say good night to Sheriff Harding."

"Good night, Sheriff." Evie yawned. "Thanks for giving me piggyback rides, and the kettle corn and the merry-go-round. And 'tecting me from the fire."

Audra ached with unfulfilled want. Carter—so near and yet untouchable.

"Anytime." Carter backed away. Soon he was merely a pale figure, striding away down the dark alley, heading back to his Jeep.

Loss whistling coolly through her, Audra turned and nudged Evie inside. "I'll get you right to bed, sweetheart. We've got a busy day tomorrow." Her cheery voice rang false to her ears.

Shirley met them in the kitchen. "Did you see Chad on your way home? He hasn't come home yet."

"No." Audra paused at these unwelcome words. "Didn't the deputies find him?"

"If they have, they haven't called me." Frowning, Shirley walked past Audra toward the back door. Then she parted the white curtains and peered out a window.

"He'll come home," Audra said, but without any real conviction. Drat the boy. Why couldn't he show some maturity?

Shirley sighed. "Like a bad penny, you mean? I keep telling myself he's come a long way this year. I'll call the sheriff's department and then try to turn Chad over to God. He can keep him safe."

As Audra passed her, she patted Shirley's shoulder. Shirley sounded as if she were trying to convince herself. Audra, a mother too, understood how hard it was to let go and let God.

And tonight Chad had stepped over the line again, but how far? Tossing firecrackers into the crowd would be just the kind of thing a liquored-up kid would do. Suddenly Audra didn't feel like the hopeful woman who'd almost kissed Carter on the back porch.

Aggravation prickled inside Audra. She marched upstairs. *Lord, You're going to have to handle all of this,* she prayed. *I can't figure out who's to blame. And please do something about my uncle. Help Carter get these fires solved soon. And bring Chad home so Shirley won't fret all night.*

Chapter 9

Early the next morning, already uncharacteristically hot, humid, and oppressive even before daylight, Audra bid a sleepy farewell to her bed. As she left the stuffy attic, she patted Evie, who was still deeply asleep. After a night of tossing and turning with nightmares of fires and Evie screaming, Audra dragged herself out of the quiet house into the unusually sticky air. Fires or no, her customers would arrive in three hours, wanting their coffee hot and their pastries sweet, flaky, and buttery. Nearing her Victorian, she scanned the charred remains of the forlorn carnival. Her gloom deepened.

When she unlocked the front door of her café and entered, Chad stepped out of the downstairs parlor. She gasped. "Chad? How did you get in?"

He motioned toward the side of the house where the wrap-around porch extended. "I climbed in a window last night."

Audra didn't like the sound of that breach of her security. Had Chad been here last evening or was he tossing firecrackers into the carnival crowd? But she only said, "I hope you locked it after yourself. I thought I had all the windows on the first floor locked."

Chad shrugged and then winced.

Audra studied him. His clothes were rumpled, his hair uncombed, almost standing up on end. Her jaw firmed. "You slept here, didn't you?"

"Yeah."

She noticed he caught himself just before he nodded again and substituted the surly "yeah." A hangover? She walked up to him and the stench of cigarettes and stale alcohol nearly gagged her. She pursed her lips. "Into the bathroom." She motioned for him to precede her down the hall behind him. Did this kid ever think first?

"Why?"

"Because I need you to work this morning and I can't stand the smell of you. You get into the bathtub and wash up. I'll call Shirley and ask her to bring over a change of clothing for you. Move it." Should she call Carter and tell him that Chad had turned up here?

She heard him mutter something like, "You're not my mother."

"No, I'm not your mother. I'm your employer and I'm teaching you that you don't show up for work in clothes you've slept in, reeking of tobacco, liquor, and body odor."

He growled something she didn't hear clearly. Fortunately. But he obeyed her. The downstairs bathroom, which customers could use, still had its original claw-foot tub.

When she stepped inside the bathroom, another unpleasant odor greeted Audra. Her hands clenched. The urge to again hit Chad over the head with a spoon—for his own good—was powerful. She gritted her teeth. "Were you sick in here?"

Chad didn't reply.

She exhaled. "Great. Just great." She sprayed air freshener. Then she showed him the high cupboard in which she'd stashed shampoo, soap, a spare toothbrush and paste, comb, and towels and left him to clean up.

She muttered all the way to the kitchen and called Shirley and told her Chad had spent the night in her Victorian and to please bring a clean set of clothing for him ASAP. After a few more comments, Audra hung up and pulled on a fresh apron. "I'm way too young to be dealing with a teenager," she grumbled to the silent kitchen.

Then she picked up the phone and dialed Carter. He needed to know about Chad. Her heightened sensitivity from last night when anticipating his kiss quivered through her. His voice came over the phone. For a moment she couldn't speak. Then she cleared her throat. "Carter, I need to tell you about Chad."

———

SHIRLEY ENDED THE CALL. Relief over finding out where Chad had spent the night vied with irritation. She couldn't seem to get through to the boy. *What should I do with him, Lord?* She mounted the flight of stairs to the second floor and tiptoed past Tom's door. She hoped he was still asleep.

Last night when he'd insisted on sitting up with her downstairs to wait for Chad, she'd realized he wouldn't rest until she did. He was still healing and needed his sleep. So she'd sent him upstairs to his room and had gone to her first-floor room. But not to sleep. After midnight, she'd crept down to the kitchen to await Chad's knock on the back door. But of course, it never came.

Now she let herself into Chad's room. It was a mess as usual and smelled of unwashed socks. She never made a big deal about the messy room, because she had more important things she needed to teach Chad first—like honesty, responsibility, and the most important—loving and being loved.

Shaking her head, she went to the stack of clean clothes she'd set on the end of his bed two days ago, which had included instructions for him to put them into his dresser in the right drawers. Her eyes gritty from lack of sleep, she exhaled loudly. Then she began picking out clean underwear, socks, and a T-shirt for him. She turned to the closet where she'd hung his blue jeans and selected a decent pair for work. Checking her armload, she gave the room one last once-over, and halted, her spirits plummeting. She'd glimpsed something she didn't want to see here. Weak-kneed, she sat down on the end of the unmade bed. *Are those what I think they are?*

———

A FEW MINUTES AFTER Shirley had come and gone, Chad joined Audra in the kitchen at the rear. His hair was still wet from his bath, but he was dressed in fresh clothing.

"Feel better?" she asked, wondering if Carter would come to pick up Chad or wait and get him at Shirley's later.

"Yeah." Without smiling, he lifted an apron off the hook on the wall.

"I've already put the first batch in the ovens," Audra said, resisting the temptation to lecture him about causing Shirley to lose sleep. She didn't envy Carter if he had to get any information out of this very surly Chad. "You can have a few rolls when they come out. That should give you some energy."

"Thanks." He headed to his workstation and began shaping dough.

He sounded subdued, but better than he had at first sight. Still, something about Shirley's expression when she'd delivered the clothing only minutes ago plagued Audra. Was it just Chad's not coming home last night? Or had something else upset Shirley?

———

JUST AFTER EIGHT O'CLOCK in the morning, Carter felt about ten years older than he had the night before the carnival. As he climbed out of his Jeep in the alley behind Shirley's house, a sharp sense of disappointment jabbed him. Last night on the back steps, Audra had nearly let him kiss her again in spite of her uncle's early-evening meltdown. How could he protect her from her uncle? With leaden dread, he mounted the back steps of Shirley's house. Shirley was waiting for him at the back door, her face twisted with anxiety. She held the door open for him.

"What is it?" he asked, sensing he wouldn't like the answer.

"Tom's still asleep." She put a finger to her lips. "Come up to Chad's room with me."

Not encouraged by her stiff tone, he followed her up and into the second-story bedroom. With each step up, his mood lowered.

She pointed and said, "There. I didn't touch them."

Carter walked over to the side of the bed Shirley had indicated, and saw firecrackers and matches. His mouth firmed into a grim line.

"Chad knows he's not to have anything like that," Shirley said, sounding near tears. "I told him no smoking, no fireworks. Nothing with matches. I told him he'd have to live down his reputation as a fire-setter and that the only way to do it was to steer absolutely clear of any hint of anything to do with fire or fireworks. We just had this conversation again a week before the Fourth."

How could Chad be this stupid? Carter turned and put a comforting arm around Shirley. "You're doing a good job with Chad. He just has a long way to come, and Doyle isn't helping."

She started to cry.

"Hey, this isn't your fault. Don't jump to conclusions." He patted her back. Shirley didn't deserve this kind of trouble.

"Shirley, just because Chad had firecrackers in his room doesn't prove that he lit any."

Shirley wiped her eyes and tried to smile. "You're right. But I know people are blaming him for the fires. Even though I've told everyone that I don't believe that Chad is responsible. They keep bringing up Doyle and his sorry reputation. As if they don't think Chad has the power to turn out different than his father."

Carter listened with only half his attention. Would he have to bring Chad in for more questioning? The fact that he had firecrackers in his room proved nothing. Unless Chad admitted setting off the firecrackers, which Carter didn't anticipate, he had nothing to link Chad to last night's fire or any of the other fires. This case was like wandering through a maze on a moonless night without a flashlight. *I have no clues to follow.* Nothing but stupid pennies. But he was the law here and he had to move forward with the investigation.

"Shirley, with your permission, I'd like to search Chad's room in case there's more evidence either to clear him or implicate him in last night's fire. Do I have your permission as the owner of this house and Chad's legal guardian?"

"Yes, you do." She walked from the room and closed the door behind her.

Carter scanned the cluttered room. He dourly pulled a pair of thin latex gloves out of his pocket and moved to one corner of the room. He began at the top of piles of magazines and CDs, lifting everything, systematically sifting for any more evidence of incendiary materials.

An hour later, Carter had finished. Nothing. He'd found exactly nothing. A brick of dissatisfaction settled in his stomach. In Shirley and Tom's presence, he bagged the firecrackers and matches and labeled them. He gave Shirley a receipt for them and left. He was glad Tom had awakened and was trying to cheer Shirley up. But Carter had to face

Chad now and find out why the kid had forbidden fire-crackers in his room.

Wilma, owner of the bed-and-breakfast near Tom's shop, hurried from her backyard and waved Carter down in the alley. He stopped his Jeep and asked, "What can I do for you, Wilma?"

"Is it true what I'm hearing about last night's fire?"

"What are you hearing?" He tried to sound completely professional.

"That Chad Keski caused a fight at the carnival and then came back later and threw firecrackers into the crowd. Was anyone hurt in the fire?"

Carter felt like grinding his teeth. He'd hoped for a little time before accusations were leveled, but Winfield's rumor mill had evidently been busy all night. "No one was injured beyond a few bumps and bruises, which resulted from the crowd panicking. And I have no evidence to connect Chad or anyone else to the fire last night."

Wilma folded her arms. "I don't want to make trouble for that kid, but my guests were at the carnival and fireworks last night. They were really shook up when they got back. I sat up with them for a long time, calming them down. Nothing like this has ever happened here. People come here to relax. They don't want to be afraid that they'll wake up and find my bed-and-breakfast in flames."

"I'm doing my best, Wilma."

"Well, your best better improve." Huffing, Wilma turned and walked away.

Carter didn't blame her. The fires were getting more dangerous. He couldn't even be sure that the firecrackers last night were connected to the previous four fires—the first at Ollie's convenience store, then Shirley's back porch, Audra's mother's shed, and Tom's shop. Bitter acid reflux scalded his throat.

He couldn't accuse Chad of anything. Owning firecrackers was not a crime. He'd just disobeyed his foster mother. What to do? Carter drove to Audra's and parked in the alley behind her café. He approached the open Dutch door and looked in. Part of him hummed to life. *Audra is here.* But duty shouldered past this flash of elation. Shirley had done her civic duty calling him to tell him about Chad and now he was forced to come here as follow-up, not because he wanted to see Audra. But he didn't want to rile Chad and perhaps trigger more self-destructive behavior or cast more suspicion on him. *How should I handle this kid?*

Chad was taking a tray of rolls out of the oven. The delicious smell of baking breads and sweets drifted to Carter, making his mouth water and his empty stomach rumble. He focused on his reason for coming, marshaling his wits. Before he dealt with Chad, he wanted to speak to Audra. Again, the image of her face lifted to his, her soft lips parted, flowed warmly through him. Carter waited until Chad set the baking sheet on the counter before announcing his presence. "Chad, where's your boss?"

Chad looked up and managed to combine both guilt and belligerence in a single glance. "She's out front." He spat out the words. "Making coffee."

With a curt nod, Carter let himself in and walked through the kitchen to the front foyer. There, Audra was completely involved in operating the growling coffee machine.

For a moment, forgetting his mission, he just enjoyed gazing at her. He took in her fair hair twirled into a tight knot at her nape, her slender shoulders, and crisp white apron. Her unadorned beauty suddenly rendered him tongue-tied. "Good morning," he managed to say past the lump around his Adam's apple.

Audra gave a little jump and turned toward him. Her unnerved expression reminded him of how she'd looked on the night she rushed him out of her kitchen when the phone rang. He still had to find out who was calling and upsetting her. Could there be some connection between the calls and the fires?

"Good morning," she replied with a tentative smile. "You look as though you feel as beat as I do."

Resisting the urge to draw her into his arms, he made a sound of amused displeasure. "It was a long night." And he didn't sleep much of it. He stiffened himself against her appeal and asked, "When does Chad get off this morning?"

Her smile vanished. She eyed him. "He should be taking the final baking sheets out of the ovens now. When all the baking is done along with the cleanup of the kitchen, he's free for the day."

Carter noted she didn't ask why he wanted to know. But her large, sympathetic eyes avoided his. Did she feel guilty about calling him to report on Chad's whereabouts? "I know your coffee is better, but I'm going to take Chad over to Trina's for a full breakfast. I need to talk to him about last night."

Her brow furrowed. "He slept here last night."

"Oh. Shirley called me about something else."

"Shirley?" Her blue eyes connected with his.

"Yes." He said no more. Chad might be listening and, after all, he never discussed cases unless necessary.

Audra studied him as if trying to read more from his words. "Will I see you later?"

Carter hesitated, wanting to assure her. "Would it be okay if I called you later?"

She nodded, looking quietly pleased.

He wished he could make her smile again. But the weight of trying to help Chad dragged at him.

He said good-bye and then walked back through the kitchen. He stopped and stared at the kid, waiting for Chad to acknowledge him.

Chad looked up suspiciously. "What's going on?"

"Finish up getting the baked goods ready," Carter ordered, "and then I'm taking you to breakfast at Trina's. I'll be waiting for you in my Jeep. You can come back here after breakfast and do the cleaning then." Carter didn't wait for a response, but walked to the Dutch door.

Chad didn't look as if he had the energy to make a break for it. In fact, he looked hungover. Maybe that would teach him to leave alcohol alone.

His own past sins stung Carter's conscience. From the time he was fifteen, he'd been drunk every weekend—until that fateful night at a party in the local state forest campground, he'd hit another kid on the head with a full beer bottle and nearly killed him. That night Carter had learned first-hand how fear and self-disgust could overwhelm a person. The memory still had the power to grip him. How could he help Chad see that being drunk was not cool and could lead to dangerous behavior before the boy made a mistake that could ruin his life?

———

THREE BLOCKS AWAY FROM the wharf, Trina's Good Eats was an institution in Winfield. The current Trina's grandmother had opened it in 1927. Trina's served generous breakfasts and homemade pasties—those flaky pastry pockets filled with beef, gravy, and veggies for lunch. Trina's had never known a day lean of customers. It opened at six o'clock, six days a week, year-round, and closed at two o'clock every afternoon. Trina never advertised. Smart tourists found it on their own. In the summer, the regulars only mildly resented strangers when they found them occupying their accustomed booths. After all, allowances had to be made during tourist season.

The 1927 bell above Trina's door jingled when Carter led Chad inside. All eyes turned toward them, as was to be expected. After nodding generally, Carter looked over everyone's heads and led Chad to an empty booth near the back. The mixed aromas of maple syrup, bacon, and butter hung appetizingly in the air. Carter hoped this setting would loosen Chad's tongue and make the kid listen to some good advice.

Carter slid into the booth, facing the door, and Chad slid in across from him. The booth was the original high-backed dark wood bench with a worn matching table. Tourists considered the vintage 1920s decor a big part of the Trina's dining experience. A decade ago, a food columnist had written about Trina's in the *Milwaukee Journal,* and Trina had framed and hung the now-yellowed column prominently near the cash register.

Carter sensed a subtle shift in the restaurant's atmosphere. Winfield was processing his bringing Chad here and not to the police station.

The now-presiding Trina, a thin blonde in her middle years wearing blue jeans, a denim vest, and a red-and-white-striped blouse, brought over menus and offered him coffee. He nodded and she turned over his mug and filled it.

Chad spoke up. "I'll have some, too,"

"How about a cup of coffee and a tall glass of orange juice, Chad?" Carter suggested, hoping to get the kid hydrated.

"Okay," Chad muttered.

Trina provided Chad with coffee and turned away "Coming right up." Trina's red plastic bangle bracelets clacked together as she walked toward the counter.

Carter opened the menu out of habit though he knew what he wanted already. Had this been a good idea or not? He prayed for wise words. "What are you in the mood for, Chad? My treat."

"What do you want?" Chad asked in an undertone.

"Right now—" Carter closed his menu and put it down "—breakfast and some information."

A hunted look flared in Chad's eyes.

No, this wasn't going to be easy or pleasant. Carter picked up his cup.

With the coffeepot in one hand, Trina appeared with a tumbler full of orange juice in the other. "You two ready to order?"

"I'll have the Fisherman's Special," Carter said.

"Me too," Chad muttered, his stomach suddenly growling loud and clear. The teen colored. He looked away.

Carter recalled being that young and so painfully insecure, like living with an exposed nerve. Or two.

Trina took the menus. "That was some commotion last night, Sheriff. Did anyone get hurt?"

Chad looked up, a question in his expression.

"No, no one was hurt," Carter replied, keeping irritation out of his voice. Trina had every right to question him about public safety. "I'm still investigating."

"That makes five fires since Memorial Day weekend started," Trina commented.

Carter was aware that most conversations around their booth had faded away. "I'm aware of that, Trina," he said mildly. Did everyone think he was enjoying these fires?

"There was another fire?" Chad asked in a thin voice.

"Yes," Carter answered before Trina could. "After the fireworks last night someone threw firecrackers into the crowd and started a few of the booths on fire."

Chad looked as though someone had punched him in the stomach.

"Well, I hope," Trina said, "that you arrest this arsonist before some tourist gets hurt. We don't need this kind of stuff getting on the news—you know in Milwaukee or Chicago news."

Chad's hands resting on top of the table became fists.

"Everything that can be done is being done," Carter said in a tone of finality. Trina and Wilma were only voicing what he'd expected, what he'd said to himself. The fires had to be stopped. And it was up to him to make it happen.

"Okay." Trina walked away and began refilling coffee cups on her way to put in their order. Conversations around Carter and Chad buzzed back to life. Carter had no doubt that last night's fire, the previous fires, and now Carter's overheard words would continue as the topics of discussion.

"Is that why you invited me to breakfast?" Chad hissed. "Because you think I set another fire? I was passed out drunk last night. I didn't even hear the fireworks." He lowered his head into one hand.

Carter viewed the teen over the rim of his heavy mug. "Chad, believe it or not," he said in a low voice only for the kid, "I'm trying to keep you from being railroaded."

Chad's head snapped up and his mouth dropped open. "What? Why?"

"Because I think it's just too convenient." As Carter spoke, the truth of what he was saying became stronger in his mind. "With your past, you're the perfect scapegoat, and I don't buy solutions that are too easy."

This closed Chad's mouth. He picked up his orange juice and drained half of it. "Then why did you bring me here?"

"Partly to keep from calling you into the station for questioning and partly to show the town that I don't consider you a suspect."

"You can't make me believe that you don't think I'm the one setting all these fires."

"If I believed that"—Carter put down his coffee cup— "you'd be at the station in a cell." He hoped that sounded serious enough to frighten Chad into telling the truth.

Trina delivered their platters of buttered toast, scrambled

eggs, golden hash browns, four strips of crisp bacon, and four links of sausage. "These breakfasts will stick with you a lot longer than those fancy rolls at Audra's." Grinning, Trina didn't sound aggrieved. She was teasing him now.

Chad picked up his fork. His expression made it obvious that the overflowing platter had instantly absorbed all of his attention.

Carter gave Trina a look he hoped told her nothing.

"But of course, Sheriff," Trina continued in that sly voice, "you get Audra's pretty face along with coffee and rolls." Giving Carter a knowing look and a wink, Trina poured more coffee for Carter and some for Chad and walked away.

Carter felt his neck warm. He tried to look unfazed but Trina's words had hit their mark. He and Audra were definitely on the gossip train in town.

"What was that all about?" Chad asked belatedly around a mouthful of toast.

Carter shrugged. He'd expected gossip if he showed interest in Audra. But he knew clearly now, no matter what, he wasn't going to stop trying to get closer to her. This decision steadied him.

Carter began eating. He decided to use the public nature of this interview to his advantage. Perhaps it would help him get facts from Chad without all the backtalk and guff. "Now I don't want you to fly off the handle in here. I need to ask you some questions and I don't want a public scene. We don't need to give the gossips any more to work with. Okay?"

Chad chewed and swallowed. "Okay. You're buying."

"Glad you see it my way," Carter said, trying to lighten the conversation. "Now I know you got liquor from someone yesterday and I'm guessing it was your dad."

Chad slid forward, ready to object. "I—"

Carter interrupted, "I don't want to argue about that now. And remember, keep your cool. You can, can't you?"

"Yeah," Chad snapped sourly.

"After you had a few drinks, you and Brent exchanged words and a fight started. That much I—along with a crowd of witnesses—know to be true. When did you end up at Audra's?"

Chad chewed, taking his time answering. Then he focused on his food while speaking, "After the fight, I got sick in the alley and it made me feel..." He shrugged. "I didn't want to go home to Shirley's like that, so I went to Audra's and climbed in the window. I must have passed out then. When I woke up, it was really dark. And quiet." Chad finally looked at Carter. "How bad was the fire last night?"

Bad enough. Carter took a sip of hot coffee. "It did a lot of damage to the carnival and it scared a lot of people. You must have been really out cold not to have heard all the sirens and noise. Audra's is just down the block from all the action."

"I didn't hear anything. I was out cold. And when I woke up, I wished I hadn't. My head felt like it was going to split open."

"And you didn't go home because—"

"Because I was sick, throwing-up sick," Chad finally confessed, sounding disgusted with himself. "I didn't want Shirley to see me like that." Though his head was down, his forehead went red.

This reaction bolstered Carter's confidence that Chad wasn't setting these fires. Obviously Shirley had gotten through to Chad on some level, enough to make him care about her seeing him drunk. "Chad, don't disappear like that again. Shirley was really worried about you."

Chad shifted on his bench.

"Another reason I invited you to breakfast has to do with Shirley, too. Now I don't want you to erupt in public, right? Can you keep your cool?"

"Yeah, yeah, I can." Chad gave him a contemptuous look.

"When Shirley went to your room to get your clothes this

morning, she found firecrackers and matches on the floor on the side of your bed."

Chad half rose.

Carter pressed down hard on one of Chad's forearms. "Chill."

"I never had any firecrackers," Chad said low, but in a heated tone. "When it all went down, I was passed out inside Audra's house."

Listening to more than just the words, Carter nodded. He believed that Chad didn't want to look bad in front of Shirley. Otherwise, he'd have gone home last night. "I believe you. But that leaves us with the question of how the firecrackers and matches got into your room."

Chad settled back down on his bench seat, looking wary. "You believe me?"

Carter nodded and went on eating his way through the delicious cholesterol on his plate but barely tasting it. Time to deliver some truth to Chad. "Yes, but I still think you've been acting like an immature kid."

He held up his fork, motioning Chad not to reply. "This is what I think. I think you're stupid enough to drink alcohol from your dad, stupid enough to start a drunken brawl in public with Brent. But not stupid enough to leave firecrackers and matches lying around your room for Shirley to find."

"Thanks," Chad said sullenly. "Thanks a lot."

Carter shrugged. "Just telling the truth. Now, besides Brent, who else doesn't like you?"

Chad imitated Carter's shrug. "Does the guy setting the fires have to dislike me to do that?"

This brought Carter to a pause. "You're right. He doesn't have to dislike you to cast suspicion onto you. Chad, I'm not going to railroad you. But you need to start thinking before you act. Shirley's been good to you. And you should try to make things easier for her."

Slowly Chad nodded, his head down.

"Chad?"

"I hear you," the kid muttered.

Carter sipped his coffee.

"If I told you something, would you believe me?" Chad asked, his eyes still lowered.

"Is it true?"

"Yeah, but... You—"

"Just tell me." Carter forked in a mouthful of bacon and egg.

"Brent had firecrackers last night. I saw the end of a string of them in his pocket."

"A string of firecrackers?" Unwelcome news.

"Yeah." Chad sounded subdued.

"Did you see matches, too?"

"No, but if he had firecrackers," Chad pointed out, "he'd have matches, wouldn't he? Or a lighter?"

"Probably." Carter studied Chad's body language. Truth or lie?

"His dad was out of control last night." Chad looked up then.

"He doesn't like me," Carter deadpanned.

Chad eyed Carter, a smile tugging one corner of his mouth. "Big-time."

Carter nodded. *And it seems there's nothing I can do about it.*

"He must have had one too many, too." Chad drained his orange juice.

This opinion took Carter by surprise. Had alcohol contributed to Hal's outburst last night? Carter didn't recall smelling liquor on Ramsdel's breath, but Chad had reeked of it. That could have masked any liquor odor on Ramsdel.

"Can you get fingerprints off the stuff Shirley found?" Chad asked.

"Doubtful. Stuff was too small to get a whole print. Just partials."

Chad chewed and then said in a rush, "I would never hurt Tom." He ducked his head protectively.

"I feel the same way, Chad."

Chad met his eyes then.

"Chad, if you don't listen to anything else I tell you, listen to this. Stick with Shirley and Tom. They're good people."

"Maybe I've gone too far." Chad's face twisted. "Shirley said I couldn't keep on running away. I didn't mean to last night. It just sort of happened."

"Want my advice?"

Chad stared at him and then bobbed his head.

"After breakfast, finish up your work at Audra's. Go straight home, apologize, and tell Shirley everything about last night. And if you tell her the truth, that you didn't leave those firecrackers in your room, she'll believe you."

"Shirley's different, you know what I mean?" Chad's voice broke.

"I know what you mean. And Tom, too." And then, with a sinking feeling, he glimpsed a van passing the front window of Trina's. *Great. Just what I needed to make my day perfect.*

Chapter 10

Ater dropping Chad back at Audra's, Carter drove to his office. With a sense of looming disaster, kind of like entering a dentist's office and hearing the whine of a drill, he surveyed the scene in front of him. A reporter and cameraman waited just outside his entrance, right where he'd expected to find them. Trish was speaking to the female reporter. No chance of getting out of giving an interview. But he'd have to weigh every word he said, or endanger his investigation. Or look like an incompetent fool.

Sizing up the opposition, Carter got out of his Jeep. If the reporter, a perky little redhead in a light green blouse and darker green slacks, was older than twenty-two, he'd kiss Florence LeVesque. Would the reporter's inexperience work to his advantage or not? As he approached, he heard Trish say with some relief, "Here's Sheriff Harding now."

Hoping he exuded confidence, Carter strode up to the reporter and offered his hand. "What can I do for you?"

"I'm Shelley Hallstock from WFJW-TV in Rhinelander. We've been following reports of the string of arsons you've been having up here. We'd like a taped interview with you about the progress of your investigation. We'd like to reassure our viewers that you're busy solving the case."

We'd like to reassure our viewers. Yeah, right. But he smiled at her as if he truly were delighted to see her and said, "I'd appreciate the chance to reassure everyone, Miss Hallstock."

The young woman signaled her cameraman. She glanced around and then drew Carter over toward the squat redbrick building so he'd be recorded standing in front of the words, Winfield County Sheriff's Department. She then turned toward the camera and said, "This is Shelley Hallstock from WFJW-TV. I'm in Winfield County speaking to Sheriff Carter Harding about the events here after last night's fireworks." She turned to Carter and held her microphone toward him. "Sheriff, we've heard that last night there was a fire during the Fourth of July celebration. What happened?"

He stared into the camera. "Someone threw firecrackers into the carnival area. Unfortunately, a booth of stuffed animals and some others caught fire as a result. But no one was hurt, and the firefighters put the blaze out within minutes."

"I heard there was a stampede and some people got banged up and bruised."

Great. "There was a brief rush, but as soon as I explained the situation over my bullhorn, calm was restored." People from the nearby realty office had come out to watch the interview. *Why not call your friends and neighbors, too,* he invited silently.

"This isn't the first fire since the beginning of summer, is it?" she prompted.

"I wish I could say that it was, but no." The people from the office were muttering, leaning close to each other. Carter refused to let this get to him.

"As our viewers know from previous stories, you've been having a string of suspicious fires in Winfield this summer. What progress are you making in finding the culprit?"

"First, I'd like to make it clear," Carter said smoothly, "that the fires have been mostly nuisances—"

"Wasn't there a person injured in one?" she interrupted.

Two, actually, but he wasn't going to enlighten her. "Yes, my stepfather was burned."

"Your stepfather?" Her voice lifted in eagerness. "That makes this sound personal."

Carter shrugged. "I doubt it, since I had no such connection to any of the other fires. My investigation is ongoing, so I can't give you any particulars. I'm sure you understand that."

"Is this having any effect on Winfield's tourist trade? Earlier, I spoke to a few of the local business owners here, and they are all concerned about the effect of these fires on tourism."

Then when you showed up, they should have kept their mouths shut. Carter made himself smile politely. "I don't think any of our summer residents or visitors need to be concerned about their safety."

A car drove into the parking lot and a man got out. Carter saw with sinking spirits that it was none other than Hal Ramsdel. *Great. Just outstanding.* "None of the fires," Carter continued, "have involved any businesses such as restaurants, motels, or campgrounds that serve tourists. All the incidents have involved local people. Tourists have nothing to lose sleep about or any reason to change their vacation plans."

"But the fire last night definitely involved tourists," the reporter pointed out.

"Last night's fire was the result of someone's carelessness with firecrackers." Carter watched Ramsdel's approach.

"I see. But that leaves unsolved the previous four fires which, as you admit, have primarily affected locals. Is someone here—how shall I put it?—settling old scores with arson?"

"That could be one explanation," Carter replied, his stress rising with Ramsdel's every step toward them. Who knew what the man would open his mouth and come out with? "The two most common motives for arson are profit and revenge."

"I hear that you have a teenager in town who has a history of fire-setting."

Carter wished the good citizens of Winfield could keep their lips zipped. And Ramsdel was within hearing distance now. The more the merrier. Carter tensed, expecting the man to come charging up, naming Chad as the teenager in question. Carter tried to think of some way to avert this, but with the camera rolling, what could he say? He couldn't arrest Ramsdel for speaking to a reporter.

Carter kept his voice even, his temper on hold. "In response to that question, you understand that, by statute, I have to be very careful in speaking about suspects, especially underage ones. So I prefer to say nothing. And I would caution"—he made eye contact with the camera—"everyone to not jump to conclusions. If I had conclusive evidence against any one person, I would have already charged them."

"Well, Sheriff, people are concerned."

"My deputies and I are investigating each fire exhaustively. Unfortunately, the person setting these fires doesn't follow the same MO or pattern each time."

"You mean no two fires are alike?" She wrinkled her brow.

"Exactly. The only fact connecting them is that they've all taken place in Winfield." Ramsdel was inexorably nearing and there wasn't anything Carter could do to prevent another public scene. *Keep your cool*, he told himself. *Don't let him goad you into showing temper for the camera.*

"What about the pennies then?" the reporter asked.

Surprise rattled him. "Pennies?"

"There's a rumor that a handful of pennies has been found at the scene of each fire."

Just in time, Carter stopped himself from showing how unwelcome this news was. Who had let the pennies clue slip?

He took refuge in repeating the true but completely noncommittal statement, "I really can't comment on the specifics of an ongoing investigation. I think that's about all I can tell you, Miss Hallstock."

Ramsdel halted behind the cameraman, rocking back and forth on his heels.

Carter's jaw clenched. He caught himself and consciously relaxed his face and continued, "We're having trouble with a few arsons, but I'd like to reiterate that every tourist is safe in Winfield. They are not the target." He smiled for the camera and hoped the filming would stop now—before Ramsdel had a chance to blast off.

"Poor comfort for the rest of us," Ramsdel commented, stepping forward from the small circle of people who'd gathered to watch the interview.

Carter eyed Ramsdel.

The reporter turned and gave Ramsdel an appraising look.

"I'm Hal Ramsdel of Ramsdel Insurance Agency, one of Winfield's local businessmen," Ramsdel said. "I understand that the sheriff is faced with a difficult case."

Carter couldn't believe his ears. Ramsdel was taking great pains to sound businesslike, calm, and even diplomatic.

"But," Ramsdel cautioned, "some of us believe that this string of fires could have been solved"—he paused to give a very phony smile—"by a more competent man. Sheriff Harding has only been in office for a few months and many of us, at the time of his winning the spring election, thought Harding as sheriff would be a mistake."

Carter burned in aggravated silence. He tried to keep his expression placid and his lips together.

Even the perky redhead looked a bit nonplussed. Obviously she hadn't expected something like this. "I see," she said, evidently stalling for inspiration.

"I'm going to begin a petition to have the sheriff relieved

of his duties and another election held," Ramsdel continued. "Winfield needs someone who can solve this quickly."

Upon hearing this, the reporter was no longer at a loss. Conflict was her stock-in-trade. She swung the microphone from Ramsdel to Carter and asked, "What do you have to say to that, Sheriff?"

Carter forced his taut shoulders to relax. "I don't know if that's even a legal avenue for Mr. Ramsdel. But if he strongly feels that I should be recalled, he has every right as a citizen and resident to make his dissatisfaction public and official."

The redhead looked back and forth between the two men, looking for a way to egg more indiscreet words from them.

"I really must go on with my duties now." Carter forestalled her. "You'll have to excuse me." He nodded to the reporter, the camera, and Ramsdel and made a tactical retreat inside and shut the door. He could do nothing to silence Ramsdel, and standing there any longer would make him look less competent, not more.

Would others in town go along with Ramsdel and sign his petition? Carter's gut tightened. Yet maybe Ramsdel was right. Maybe someone else could do better, solve these fires. But Carter's instincts and training instantly denied this. No one could have done better with the paltry clues he'd found. Not even Hal Ramsdel.

Carter strode toward his office, motioning Trish to come with him. After this interview, many unanswered questions nagged him. Who had let the pennies clue slip? He'd told Audra but he trusted her implicitly so who was it? And how would Ramsdel feel when Carter questioned Brent about Chad's allegation that there had been firecrackers in Brent's pocket last night?

And what had altered Ramsdel's behavior around him? The calm, rational man who'd responded to the reporter was a completely different man than the one who'd caused an outrageous public scene last night. Was this a good sign or the portent of something worse from Ramsdel? *What gives, Lord?*

———

THE NEXT NIGHT AT TEN o'clock, Carter parked his Jeep in the alley behind Audra's Place. The unusual muggy weather had lingered, wrapping around Winfield like a warm wet compress. Off duty at last, he shed his hat and jacket and tossed them into the back. The lake breeze wafted through the car window and cooled the perspiration on his forehead.

Yesterday had only gone downhill after the TV interview and Ramsdel's appearance. Knowing that Audra wouldn't have repeated what he'd told her, Carter's dispatcher had admitted telling her sister about the pennies. He'd given her a stiff warning that another lapse would result in her losing her job, but it was too late now.

Tonight another unappealing task awaited, questioning Brent. Carter had decided instead of getting into Ramsdel's face again, a casual question to Brent at Audra's would serve his purpose of getting Brent's alibi for the Fourth of July blaze.

Also, if things fell into place, he might be able to put an end to the mystery of Audra and her unwelcome, and from the sound of them, abusive phone calls. If he couldn't solve the fires, he could at least help Audra. *Whoever you are, please call tonight while I'm there. Please.*

Along the quiet alley, Audra's Dutch door was half open to the night. White light spilled out. What must it be like working in this heat beside two commercial ovens without air conditioning? Something inside his chest tightened almost painfully. Audra deserved an easier life, one where she'd be with her daughter all day. He couldn't understand why she didn't even date. Why hadn't she married someone by now?

The question ignited an instant and intense denial within

him. He didn't want any other man in Audra's life. He got out of the Jeep. For months, he'd been telling himself that he and Audra didn't have a future. But was that true?

He walked to the door and looked inside. Brent and Audra were cleaning up after the pizza trade. Again, she looked out of place here. Her pert nose sported a dot of pizza sauce and her eyebrows had collected flour. "Good evening," he said. "My pizza ready?"

Both Brent and Audra swiveled to look at him. "Howdy, Sheriff," Brent drawled.

Audra smiled, but ducked away and wiped her face with a kitchen towel. She turned back. "Hi, it's in the warming oven."

He'd detected a special welcoming glint in her eyes just for him. Carter let himself inside. "Anything I can do to help out?"

"We're almost finished," she replied. She swept off her sauce-smeared apron and smoothed back loose golden tendrils around her face.

"Go ahead," Carter said. "I'm in no hurry." In fact, he'd ordered the pizza for them to share, to be here when another call came again.

"Saw your interview on TV last night," Brent said, baiting Carter. "Did you like my dad's idea?"

Carter ignored Brent's dig. "I don't think I have a future in television," he said dryly.

A laugh burst out of Brent. "Good one." The kid gave him a thumbs-up. "I don't think my dad has one, either."

But Carter wouldn't say something negative that Brent could repeat to his dad. Instead, he casually asked the question he'd been saving for over a day. "I hear you had some firecrackers on the Fourth of July."

"Yeah, me and most of the rest of Wisconsin. Firecrackers aren't against the law, right?" Brent taunted.

Audra looked at Brent and then Carter. "Brent, stop being

cute and tell the sheriff that you had nothing to do with the fire on the Fourth."

"I had nothing to do with the fire on the Fourth," Brent parroted and grinned.

Carter shrugged. "Fine." Brent just didn't seem worth the effort tonight. And the kid was right. Having firecrackers wasn't against the law. To make something of it, Carter would have to have a witness to Brent lighting and throwing them. Just the same as he'd need to charge Chad.

Audra studied Carter again. And then she turned to Brent. "Done?"

"Yeah, I get the hint." Smirking, Brent took off his apron, wadded it up, and tossed it like making a basket into a pile of laundry near the door. "See you tomorrow for another fun day in Winfield. I can't wait to see the second Friday in August," he said sarcastically and loped toward the door.

"You just have to ignore Brent," she said with a sigh.

"What happens the second Friday in August?" Carter asked anyway.

"He goes to spend two weeks with his mother in Chicago," Audra replied.

An unexpected voice came from just outside. "Good. I got here in time." It was Brent's dad in the doorway.

"What are you here for?" Brent asked, clearly unhappy to see his father. "I don't need you to take me home. I've got my bike. And just so you know, I'm leaving to visit Mom August tenth."

Carter moved closer so he could get a better glimpse of Hal. The man looked like he was disgruntled but was trying to hide it.

"I'm not going to discuss that now. I thought I would drive us to A&W for root beer floats."

Brent eyed his father suspiciously. "I'm not changing my mind just because you've decided to play nice."

"Come on. Let's go." Hal motioned to Brent, who obeyed warily. "Evening, Audra, Sheriff," Hal said with a courteous nod. Then Hal and Brent disappeared into the night.

Audra and Carter stared at one another, dumbstruck. She spoke first. "Did you see that?"

Carter shook his head slowly. "I thought so, but I still don't believe it." *Hal Ramsdel, polite to me?*

"What next?" Audra turned away, still shaking her head in obvious disbelief. "I'll get your pizza boxed for you."

"I was wondering if you'd eat it with me," he said in an offhand tone. "I hate eating alone." He stayed perfectly still.

Audra faced him, looking suspicious. "Did Shirley put you up to this?"

"Shirley?" he echoed.

"She's always after me to eat more. She knows making pizzas all evening takes away my appetite."

"Well," he improvised quickly, "if you're tired of pizza, I can go and pick up burgers somewhere quick."

She considered him and glanced toward the door. "No, I...this is fine. I'll have a slice with you. Then I have to get the dough machines filled and set the timers. Okay?"

"Sure?" he asked, almost not believing she'd let him persuade her so easily.

"Sure," she echoed. "Have a seat."

"Thanks." He followed her motion toward a high stool at the counter. So far so good. Now if the phone rang, he'd be ready and in position.

In spite of that, he felt himself relaxing. Being here with Audra filled some void inside him, some dark place left over from the days when he'd been young and so angry. But being near Audra also stirred him. Tonight he admitted he'd wanted to be near her. He'd resisted this yearning, just one of his many frustrations.

Audra set two plates on the work counter and pulled a

pizza from the warming tray. She handed him a can of pop and then sat down on the stool nearest him. "How are you doing after the interview? And with the investigation?" she asked, her voice resonating genuine concern.

But he saw her glance at the phone and the clock. He read the signs as unconscious indications that she, too, was expecting—fearing—another phone call. He popped open his can and swallowed a long, cold, sweet draft. "I haven't made any progress solving the fires and see no light at the end of this yet." The sad words settled over them.

Audra lifted her piece of pizza and then set it back down as if too tired to eat. "Do you have any idea why my uncle is acting the way he is?"

He didn't mistake her reason for asking. "I don't. Do you?"

"Megan let something slip this morning." A sigh escaped her lips. "It might explain it."

He motioned for her to begin eating. She did look thinner now that he really looked. She finally took a bite of pizza. He lifted up a slice and bit into it. It was crisp on the bottom and thick with luscious melted cheese on top. *Mmm.* "Yes?"

Audra swallowed and wiped her lips. "Megan said that after a phone call very late on the Fourth, my mother drove over to my uncle's. After the fireworks. And the fire. I mean, why? They've barely been on speaking terms, and I can't imagine why she would go to visit him that day and so late."

"You think she might have said something that changed his ways?" Carter watched the way Audra ate—so feminine, her long fingers moving delicately. Who was calling and upsetting her?

"I can't think of anything else that might have caused such a shift in his behavior. But it's not much to go on, is it?"

The phone rang. Carter watched her harassed gaze swing to it. In edgy silence, they both waited as the prerecorded message played and then an angry voice demanded, "Audra, pick up. This is your last chance." Audra stood up. "Or I'm coming—"

Cutting in front of her, Carter darted forward, grabbed up the phone receiver, and barked, "This is Sheriff Harding. If you do not stop calling this number and harassing Audra Blair, I will come after you with a warrant—" Carter stopped speaking since the caller had hung up.

He put the receiver back and turned to Audra. "Who has been bothering you? I want you to tell me now."

———

AUDRA COULDN'T THINK of a thing to say. How could she tell Carter? She burst into tears.

Then Carter was folding her in his arms. The past weeks fell away from her, disintegrated. Her resistance melted. Carter was holding her. Carter had defended her. Carter cared. She rose on her tiptoes and closed the scant inches that separated them.

The first touch of his lower lip grazed her upper one and made her gasp. She leaned closer. "Kiss me," she whispered. "Please."

He kissed her slowly, gently, thoroughly. She closed her eyes, letting crest after crest of sensation shudder through her. Afterward, she pressed her face into the cleft between his neck and shoulder. The logical side of her mind tried to awaken and insist she call a halt to his embrace, to the feel of his lips brushing her hair, to the delicious sensation of being held and protected within his arms. But she found that impossible.

He pulled back a fraction of an inch from her, his eyes troubled. "Who is calling and harassing you?"

She stopped his question with another kiss. She could taste the tang of pizza sauce on his lips and for some reason that drew a sigh from her.

Then she felt his lips pull away, and he gripped her gently but firmly by her upper arms and said, "I'm not going to be distracted. Who has been making you miserable?"

No. No, I don't want to face this, tell you about this. She tried to tug away from his grip.

He leaned close to her ear and whispered, "You can trust me. You can tell me. Anything."

She returned to him and buried her face in the front of his starched shirt. His touch, his understanding words, released her. Words poured out. "It's Evie's father. Don't ask me any more about him. Please." She felt him stiffen. Immediately she wished she hadn't told him the truth. She shouldn't have reminded him of her past. She straightened up, turning away, trying to get her defenses back up, trying not to let his coming rejection hurt as much as it surely would. "I'm sorry. I shouldn't have mentioned—"

"Yes, you should have." He halted her retreat, pulling her back against him. "Has he been bothering you? Why?" Again, but now from behind, he gently but firmly gripped the bare flesh of her upper arms.

His touch, his tone bolstered her. She replied, "I haven't answered the phone. I just don't want to talk to him. Hearing his voice...upsets me."

"Are these calls of his something new? Do you keep in touch with him?"

"We haven't kept in touch." Her voice was flat. "His calling me is new this summer. I can't figure it out. Unless it has...to do with his getting married this year. But that doesn't make any sense."

"How often has he called? Has he threatened you specifically?"

"I think he flies back and forth with his father in their private plane to Chicago. They have a brokerage firm there.

He calls me a couple of times a week. His new wife is staying up north all summer at his family's cottage."

"I don't want you to agonize about this anymore," Carter ordered. "I will take care of it."

She wanted to let him, but should she? *Shouldn't I be able to handle Gordon by myself?* She moved away from Carter, sat back down on the high stool and then rested her head in her hands. *I don't want to handle Gordon by myself and that's the truth.* The elation she'd felt moments ago left her, draining her, drawing her down. "Sometimes...it's just...everything's too much. And I wish I could take a break, you know? Just get away."

"Okay. Let's do it. Let's take a break together."

Startled, she looked up at him. "What?"

"Throw that pizza into a box. And we'll escape to the beach for a one-hour vacation. It should be quiet now, and we can picnic and walk along the sand. And forget everything."

She almost refused but then she looked into his green eyes, eyes that begged her to agree. He truly felt exactly as she did. And he was right. Wouldn't it be wonderful to run away for just a little while?

Within minutes, they'd packed the pizza and extra pop and were out the door and into his Jeep. He drove them through the quiet dark streets out of town along the shore of Lake Superior. Finally, he pulled off at a deserted stretch of beach. She walked beside him, feeling the lake breeze ruffle her hair. After the heat and humidity of the long day, the cooling breeze from the lake freed her, revitalizing her. She sank down, not caring about getting sandy. She opened the box and offered it to him. "Let's eat before it's stone cold."

He lifted a slice and like someone in a pizza commercial, bit into it. "Yum."

She giggled. And the giggle released the last of her pressure. *We are free for this hour.* She lifted her arms as if reaching for the moon and stars.

Evidently feeling the same abandon, he reclined on one arm as if he were an ancient Roman emperor while she sat cross-legged like a shy maiden. The nearby waves lapped the sand. Pizza sauce oozed out onto the corner of his mouth. It made her giggle, and she wiped it away with her paper napkin. This innocent, private hour didn't count. This time was just for them. Together.

While the pizza disappeared, they talked about childhood days at the beach and sand castles and the popular sport of hunting agates on the beach. Seagulls that should have been settled for the night appeared, bobbing and pecking at the few crusts in the box.

Carter scattered the rest onto the sand and then tossed the crumpled box and cans into a trash can. He gathered her shoulders under one arm and led her to the water's edge. Silver moonlight rippled over the lake and in the distance backlit the outlines of the Apostle Islands and one of the iconic light-houses. She slipped out of her sandals and left them behind, just beyond the reach of the waves. The sand was cool and wet and squished between her toes.

He led her down the beach. In the darkness, the town lights glowed to the north, but only the sound of an occasional car traveling the highway reminded them that they weren't alone, completely set apart.

"This is the first time I've been to the beach all summer," she murmured guiltily. "Evie and I usually go to the beach every nice day in the summer."

"Let's bring her here Monday when you don't have to work."

His invitation took her by surprise. There was a self-conscious silence.

"Forget I said it," he muttered, sounding hurt. He looked around. "I should be getting you back. It's late."

No. Not yet. She reached out and took his hand and tugged

him back to her. "Evie would love to come to the beach on Monday with you. And so would I."

"I should stay away from you." He gazed over her head, not meeting her eyes.

Her pulse quickened. No. At this moment, she could believe anything was possible. Even for them. She decided to head into the wind. "Because of Sarah? Because of my uncle? You know I don't believe what my uncle says about you and Sarah."

He didn't answer her, just settled his chin on the top of her head.

She wasn't afraid tonight; tonight she could ask him anything. "Or is it because of Evie? Is it because I have a child?"

He pulled her to him, tight against him. "You know that doesn't matter to me. You're a good woman. You were young, innocent and trusted the wrong man. But that gave you Evie. She's the sweetest."

"You're a good man." Couldn't they put their pasts behind them and start anew? Together? "You just made a mistake, too, that night."

"It's not the same, Audra. You made one mistake. I made a hundred—"

"Stop. God makes all things new. I believe that, don't you?"

"God forgives, but people don't." He held her in place, not letting her step back and look up into his face.

She let him hold her. "Should we let them keep us apart? I've waited so long for someone..." She rubbed her face against his crisp shirt. Her cheek touched a sharp edge of his badge. She shouldn't say what she was thinking and feeling, should she? She couldn't say that she'd been waiting for someone to love her for herself and love her daughter for the same reason.

Within his arms, he stroked her back. "I know all about how you came to live with Shirley."

"You mean like everyone in Winfield?" The friction of his palms warmed her.

"I know it hasn't been easy. I admire you."

"I admire you," she echoed him in all sincerity.

"I've told myself over and over again not to want to be with you. But it just doesn't work." He kissed her hair, once, twice. "When this is over, when I've solved the fires, and we have time, I want us to be together, to spend time together alone and together with Evie. I'm not saying this very well, but is there a chance for me? With you?"

He'd spoken the words she thought she might never hear, the words she'd longed to hear him say. "Yes." Audra couldn't say more. Her throat was thick with emotion and she only wanted to nestle in Carter's strong arms and forget everything else.

But her mind replayed what he'd said, "When this is over, when I've solved the fires, and we have time." *Lord, let that time come soon. Please.*

Chapter 11

Four weeks to the day from the last fire, the beginning of August, Carter sat dismally at his desk near noon. Across from him sat Roger Smith, an officer from the state fire marshal's office. They both stared at the few sealed labeled bags filled with scraps of evidence, including four with blackened pennies, and the crime scene reports for each of the five fires, lying on the desktop. Each bag of pennies and each report mocked Carter.

"Let's go over this one more time," Smith suggested.

Carter picked up the yellow legal pad beside his right hand and began reading aloud:

"Fire one. Location, Ollie's store. Arsonist's motive? Unknown or maybe a test run? MO? Trip wire and incendiary pack under dumpster lid. Opportunity? Everyone in Winfield with a bike or car. No clues save a handful of blackened pennies."

"Check," Smith said as he marked something down on the notebook he'd brought along.

"Fire two. Shirley Johnson's back steps and porch," Carter continued. "Motive? Anyone with a grudge against anyone living in Shirley's house, which includes Tom Robson, Shirley, Audra and Evie Blair, and Chad Keski. MO? Gasoline-soaked steps ignited by Molotov cocktail. Opportunity? Chad had run away the night before and everyone in Winfield had opportunity in the dark alley. No clues save more pennies." Carter glanced up at Smith who marked something down and nodded again.

"Fire three. Lois Blair's garden shed," Carter read on. "Motive? Chad didn't want to do yard work—weak. MO? Long slow fuse to dry grass and twigs and gasoline-soaked rags. Opportunity? Chad Keski could have set it or anyone else. Pennies found." Carter lifted his eyes for Smith's approval, received it, and continued.

"Fire four. Tom Robson's garage. Motive? Unknown, though Tom had docked Chad's pay and Doyle Keski, Chad's father, has a grudge against both Shirley and Tom over losing custody of Chad. MO? Another trip wire, which ignited cans and bottles of gasoline products. Opportunity? Anyone. Pennies found again."

Smith grunted and Carter took that to mean to go on.

"Fire five. Downtown during the Fourth of July festivities. Motive? Unknown though preceded by Chad Keski-Brent Ramsdel brawl. MO? Firecrackers. Opportunity? Anyone present. No pennies found," Carter concluded.

Carter had written this list over and over during the past four weeks, four weeks without fire number six. Every time he'd hoped for inspiration, a flash of intuition—anything.

Smith cleared his throat. "The lack of hard evidence is probably due to the nature of the crime. Fire burns up evidence. That's another of the traditional motives for arson. Fire can cover up another crime."

Carter knew all this, but refrained from pointing that out. "But there was no evidence of a previous crime at any of the five fire scenes."

"I know, and the changing MOs made it impossible for you to chase down the source of the materials used to start each fire."

"Right," Carter agreed. "And in each case, the arsonist has used the site to his advantage, using on-site flammables so he's left no trail of materials acquisition to trace."

"And with the Internet, someone could get almost anything via mail order without calling any attention to themself," Smith said, sounding disgusted. "And for motive, there isn't a consistent one."

Carter didn't mention that Audra had suggested that she was the target since everyone, except for Ollie, was close to her. He didn't feel guilty about not mentioning this. Her theory didn't hold water, either, because the arsonist remained silent about his reasons and victims.

"Too bad we don't have any eyewitnesses," Smith commented. "Without one, there's no way to limit the suspects or even come up with a sensible list."

Carter agreed silently. It was all a mishmash of grudges and guesses. If only Florence had put on her glasses before she looked out to see who was breaking glass bottles in the alley!

"And what has put an abrupt stop to the fires?" Smith asked. "Five fires in a little over four weeks and now four weeks without another. What sense does that make?"

"It makes no sense to me." Carter rubbed his eyes with the heels of his palms. "The only thing that linked the fires is the pennies, but none were found at the Fourth of July carnival."

"Maybe the fires were set by someone who had come as a tourist and spent a month here, setting fires, and then just went home?" Smith offered.

Carter shook his head. "I find that impossible to believe."

Smith made a sound of disgust, snapped his notebook shut, and rose. "You've done everything by the book. Let us know if you get number six."

Carter rose to shake hands. "Will do. But I hope there won't be a number six." Was the rash of fires over or not? Was there a grand finale looming ahead?

A tap on his office door and then Tom leaned in. "Have time to talk? Oh, sorry."

"Come on in." Out of habit, Carter laid his legal pad face-down over the crime scene reports. "This is Roger Smith from the Wisconsin fire marshal's office. He's just leaving for Madison. My stepfather, Tom Robson."

Smith acknowledged Tom with a curt nod. "Sorry it took us so long to get up here." Smith repeated the same line he'd said when he'd arrived four hours ago, and then departed. Tom entered and sat in the chair on the other side of Carter's desk. He declined Carter's offer of coffee. "I won't beat around the bush, Son."

Tom's calling him son always lifted Carter's spirits—no matter what the situation. And after four hours of grilling by Smith, he felt better. His stepdad still looked battered and reddened from the fire. *Lord, how can I help Tom? I owe him so much.*

"Old Bilson called me and asked me to come and talk things over with you informally. He said if he came to your office in person, it would be all over town by suppertime. And the rumor mill would have a heyday."

"What did our esteemed village chairman want to discuss with me?" Carter asked, already guessing the reason.

"The fires, of course. And Hal Ramsdel's petition to have you recalled."

"I figured." Carter nodded, sour acid moving up his throat. "Okay, what else does Bilson want to warn me about that I already know?"

"Ramsdel took the effort to get everything about the petition done according to law. He's been making the rounds of local people and the summer people who've retired up here and can vote."

"I take it he's getting signatures?" Carter picked up his ball-point pen and jabbed his blotter.

"Well, right after the fire on the Fourth, he got a few locals to sign. They were worried this was going to go on all summer and affect their businesses."

"I see." Carter began making Xs on his blotter with deep slashing strokes.

"But when one, two, and now four weeks passed with no further fires, the local people have decided that it must have been some kind of fluke," Tom said. "Or done by someone not from around here—"

"I thought of that, but that doesn't jibe with the targets," Carter objected. "Why would a stranger target Lois, Shirley, and you?" Carter tossed the pen down.

"Well, it hasn't gone unnoticed that Doyle Keski quit his job and took off again. That coincided with the fires stopping. People around here think he had good motives to set the fires, motives that would make sense to someone like Doyle." Tom shook his head. "He hates Shirley for taking in Chad, and he was mad about Chad having to work for Lois. He resents my relationship with Chad, too."

"That all makes sense, but I don't have any evidence to link Doyle with any one of the fires, let alone all of them."

"I know. But Doyle's skipped and the fires have stopped. People have made the connection between the two—right or wrong." Tom shrugged.

"So people are losing interest in the petition?" Carter tried to hold back any flicker of relief.

Tom propped his elbows on the chair arms. "Some. Some not. Bilson seems to think Ramsdel has gotten quite a few retirees to sign the petition. People who don't know you."

And I'm sure Hal's given them his view of my character, Carter added silently.

"Anyway, Bilson expects Ramsdel to bring the matter up at the August county board meeting tomorrow night." Tom stared at Carter.

"Thank Bilson for the warning. But this won't be over until I solve the fires or we see they've ended for good."

"One other thing, Son. Some people heard about Shirley finding firecrackers in Chad's room—"

"How did they hear about that?" Carter sat up straighter. "Shirley didn't tell anyone, did she?"

"I think that someone might have overheard you talking to Chad that morning you took him to breakfast."

"Overheard me?" Carter shoved his chair backwards. "I don't see how anyone could have heard a thing I said to Chad. I was talking very low, and you know how noisy Trina's is in the morning."

Tom shook his head. "Anyway, if Doyle hadn't left town and the fires hadn't stopped, you would have gotten flack for playing favorites. A lot of people don't think Chad will be able to break free of the sad pattern set by his father and grandfather. You know, 'the acorn doesn't fall far from the tree' bit."

The injustice of this hit Carter and his mouth twisted down. "Just like they thought about me when I was Chad's age?"

Tom nodded, frowning. "Unfortunately, yes. In fact, Bilson had the nerve to say that people think you probably wanted to shield Chad because he's going the same way you did at that age."

"Well, I can't argue with that." With effort, Carter kept his voice even. He sincerely hoped Chad wouldn't still be living down his young mistakes twenty years from now. "I want to see Chad break the chain and be...free, free to have a good life."

Carter paused and changed topics. "How is your insurance claim going?"

"It's going. Don't worry about it. You've got enough on your plate." Tom rose and rested a hand on Carter's shoulder. "I know you're doing your best, Son. I'll be going now. I conveyed to you what Bilson asked me to and I know you have work to do." He turned toward the door.

Carter blurted out, "Do you think this reformed act of Ramsdel's is real?"

Tom grimaced. "Obviously, you don't. I don't know what to think of it. But it really doesn't ring true. Hal needs God and doesn't realize that. I..." Tom closed his lips. "Watch your back, Son. That's my advice."

"I will, Tom. I will." Carter squeezed Tom's hand on his shoulder and then let it go.

Tom waved and left, closing the door behind him.

Carter turned his legal pad over and gave a sound of disgust. *Lord, I'm at a total loss as to who's responsible for these fires. Where do I go from here?* But he'd been muttering this prayer for weeks without a hint of inspiration.

He wanted the fires to be over, but what if he never did find out who had set them? That fate seemed almost as bad as having fire number six occur tomorrow and right here in his office. He pushed himself to his feet. He'd put this out of his mind and get on with the day.

Then a pleasant thought fought its way to the front of the line. He had a date to walk the beach with Audra tonight. Ever since their first "escape," every night after she closed up, he'd stopped by and they spent some time together. They didn't walk the beach for very long, because Audra had to rise so early. But those few moments with Audra were as precious as gold and diamonds to him. More precious.

THAT AFTERNOON, JUST before four o'clock, Audra walked downstairs in her Victorian, yawning a bit from her brief afternoon nap on an air mattress she'd put upstairs. She walked into her kitchen, washed her hands, and checked the dough machines to see how the pizza dough looked. Great. Ready to start another evening's pizza trade, she slipped an apron over her head and unlocked the rear Dutch door.

Usually Brent would be lounging at the door when she opened up. But not today. She glanced down the alley right and then left. Brent wasn't in sight. She shrugged and began going through the routine, first preheating the two ovens. Soon the phone was ringing with customers ordering pizzas, but there was still no Brent.

Finally, at quarter to five, after looking up and down the alley again, Audra called her uncle's home. No answer. She left a message on the machine, asking Brent to come to work right away. *What do I do now? I can't do the pizza trade by myself.*

The phone rang again, but it wasn't Brent with an excuse and apology. Instead, she wrote down another pizza order. The mounting list of orders made the decision easy for her. She picked up the phone and asked Shirley to send Chad over ASAP.

Within just a few minutes, she heard a bicycle pull up beyond the Dutch door and then Chad strolled inside. "What's up?"

"Brent didn't show." Audra gave Chad a grateful look. "Wash up and get over here so I can show you how to work the dough for pizzas. Please."

Chad obeyed and was soon tossing pizza dough.

"That's good. You're really learning how to work with dough," Audra commented. "You should think about food service as a career."

Chad colored with pleased embarrassment, but made no reply.

Audra let herself sigh with relief. She wouldn't obsess about Brent. He was probably just off having fun somewhere and lost track of time. The phone rang again, and as she jotted down yet another order, she let go of the problem of where Brent was.

Nearly two hours later, Audra was just taking payment for three pizzas when she heard a squeal of tires and a commotion in her backyard. She thanked the customer, who lifted his three boxed pizzas and stepped away. Audra looked out the door and saw her uncle dragging Brent by the collar toward her. The customer made a hurried retreat, detouring around Hal. Audra envied him.

Another family storm was on her doorstep. Her uncle was red in the face and Brent was snarling at him. She glanced back at Chad. "Don't let Brent get to you. Please," she said under her breath. She then turned to face her family.

"Audra, I was late getting home," her uncle declared. "After I listened to the answering machine, I went upstairs and"—he shook Brent by the shoulder—"found this one playing computer games!"

Brent wrenched free. "I told you I'm quitting—"

"No, you're—"

Audra spoke over both of them—loudly, firmly, and with authority. "This is a place of business. I can't have a family fight taking place here with customers coming and going." She surprised them both into silence. They stared at her. "Now, Brent, why are you quitting? Weren't you going to work until the tenth?"

Her uncle started to reply, but she held up a hand like a referee. "Brent?"

"Mom called and said she's had a change in schedule and wants me to come early to visit her. She's going to drive up and get me this Saturday, so I can have more time with her back at home *where I belong*." He cast a fiery glance at his father.

"You have an obligation to finish the summer rush season with Audra," Hal insisted.

"But if Aunt Mary wants Brent—" Audra cut in.

"Don't call her that," Hal barked. "Mary isn't your aunt anymore—"

"But if Aunt Mary," Audra persisted, "wants Brent with her, I'll just find someone else—"

"I won't let her change the court's decision. She has Brent for two weeks in the summer and one weekend a month during the school year. That's what she agreed to—"

"Uncle Hal." Audra tried to interrupt him, stop him from doing further damage to his relationship with his son. And failed.

He talked over Audra. "Mary took me to the cleaners, but I told her, you can't have everything. If you make me sell everything now when the market's so bad, I get Brent. Not you—"

Brent turned and charged off into the twilight.

"Brent!" Audra called after him.

"Go ahead and run!" Hal bellowed. "I'm not letting her change our agreement! If she'd wanted you more than the money, she should have said so in court!"

For a split second, Audra wanted to grab Hal and shake him. How could he be so insensitive, especially humiliating Brent in front of Chad? She drew in a deep breath. "You shouldn't have said that to Brent," she snapped, bridling. "Whatever Aunt Mary's faults are, Brent is her son and he loves her."

"The divorce was all her fault—"

"Yeah," Chad spoke up from behind Audra. "Right. Not your fault at all. Nothing ever is."

Hal glared at Chad and then called the teen several names. Chad yelled back that Hal should shut his face.

"Uncle Hal—" Audra began, drawing herself up for a fight.

Hal swung away from her, still cursing and raging. Audra stepped away from the Dutch door. Her stomach shook.

"Hey, don't let that old man upset you," Chad said sympathetically.

She pulled out a stool and sat down. Her heart pounded and she felt a little sick. "Why doesn't he understand? Why doesn't he show any concern for Brent's feelings? And what makes him think he has the right to call you those terrible names?"

Chad came over, wiping his hands on his apron, and patted her back awkwardly. "Hey, don't let it get you down. I've been called worse. And by my old man, too."

The phone rang, beckoning her. Audra nodded up at Chad, wishing she could somehow make up for his father. But she could do very little. She squeezed his doughy hand. "Thanks for helping out." Then taking a deep breath, she reached for the ringing phone.

"Hey, no problem. I can use the money." He cast another dark glance at the Dutch door. "And they say my dad's a loser. Sheesh."

Audra put it all aside and greeted her customer over the phone. Even as she automatically took the order, her mind drifted off to Carter. He was coming again this evening. His late-night visits had become her reward at the end of each day. What a comfort to have him to talk to, to share her concerns. She'd only had Shirley before. *Now I have Carter.* This thought lifted her and terrified her at the same time. It was almost too good to be true.

She hung up and glanced at the clock. It was seven-thirty. Only a few more hours and he'd be here. Her lips tingled in anticipation. *Only two hours and he'll be kissing me hello.* She blushed and hoped Chad didn't notice.

A LITTLE AFTER NINE-FIFTEEN, Chad finished washing his hands at the sink.

From behind him, Audra patted him on the shoulder. "Thanks for coming right away. I couldn't have handled everything on my own."

"No problem. Should I come tomorrow at four again?"

Audra bit her lower lip. "Yes, if Brent shows, I'll send you home, but I'll pay you for an hour's time for coming, okay?"

"Hey, you don't have to pay me just to bike down a few blocks to find out if you need me."

Audra squeezed his shoulder. "'A workman is worthy of his hire.'"

"What?"

"It's from the Bible. It means a person who works should be respected and paid."

"It says that in the Bible?" Chad lifted his eyebrows. "It talks about getting paid?"

Audra nodded.

"Tom and Shirley are really into the God thing, aren't they?" Chad commented offhandedly.

She grinned. "Yes, and aren't we lucky that they are?"

This seemed to hit Chad. He stared at her a moment before replying, "I guess."

"You did a good job tonight."

Chad brushed off her compliment with a shrug and then exited through the Dutch door.

"Chad, what are you doing here?"

Audra heard Carter asking the question.

"Audra will fill you in. What're you doing here?" Chad asked slyly.

"None of your business."

Chad chuckled and Carter stepped inside and shut the door behind him.

Without hesitation, Audra went to him and twined her arms around his neck. "Carter, I—"

He interrupted her with a kiss.

She didn't mind his interruption at all. When he finally released her, her body bubbled with joy. Nothing was wrong when Carter was with her. A faint warning persisted, whispering through her. But she turned away from it.

Carter set a bulging white bag on the counter. "Hope you're in the mood for burgers tonight."

The aroma of burgers with grilled onions, her favorite, wafted to her. "Mmm, I hope you got me fries, too." She sat down, eager as a little girl. "I'm starving and I can't face another pizza."

He chuckled and sat down on the stool next to hers. They held hands and he said grace. Afterward he kissed her hand and then pulled a french fry from the bag and fed it to her.

She giggled. For a few moments, they ate in silence. Audra reveled in the wonderful feeling of being with this special man. *I'm not alone anymore.*

Then he asked, "Now tell me why Chad was here and Brent wasn't."

Audra's mood lowered a fraction. She sighed. "My uncle is such a—"

"Jerk?" Carter offered.

"I'm sorry, but yes." She went on to fill Carter in on the scene that had taken place earlier. He gave her his full attention. She voiced her concern, "Why doesn't my uncle realize how much damage he's doing to his son, to his relationship with him?"

"He's blind to his own faults." Carter set down his burger.

Even as she talked, she pored over his face, noting the laugh lines around his eyes and the deep tan of his face and neck, even the faint scar above his eyebrow.

Audra pictured her uncle, her two ex-aunts, Brent, and

then finally Sarah. "I was so little when Sarah died, just about Evie's age. Did he act the same way with her?" She caught herself. Should she have brought Sarah up?

Carter's mouth turned down. He looked away as if he were peering into the past. "I didn't see them together much—your uncle and Sarah. But she didn't have anything good to say about him." Carter shook his head. "In any event, the crowd we were running with at the time—none of the kids were happy with their parents. Including me. I don't know how Tom went on loving me anyway." Carter fell silent.

To comfort him, Audra ran her hand up his arm, feeling the latent power there. "I've been praying that my uncle would wake up before it's too late. Before he alienates his son completely."

Carter lifted her hand from his short sleeve and held it. "He's in a lot of pain himself and he isn't letting God shine truth into his life. He's blundering around in the dark, destroying relationships, causing pain. I know how that feels myself. Bad. Very bad. Did you ever ask your mother about why she visited him on the Fourth?"

"Yes. She said she'd received a call from a longtime neighbor who told her exactly how Hal had behaved at the carnival."

"So?"

"So she went over there and told him if he had to act 'the boorish lout' that he should do it in private." Audra paused. "She threatened to call his ex-wife and tell her how Hal was treating Brent and encourage her to challenge the custody agreement."

Carter whistled. "Whoa. Your mother goes right for the throat, I see."

"I'm a little proud of her for defending Brent." Audra felt a smile take over her mouth.

Carter nodded. "I think the petition drive added to his

reformed behavior. He wouldn't be able to get any signatures if he continued acting like a raving lunatic."

"Don't worry about that stupid petition. Or the board meeting coming up." She leaned forward and as naturally as it was with Evie, she kissed him.

He held her face gently in his hands and returned her kiss with dividends and interest. She longed to tell everyone that Carter cared for her. But so far it was all too special, too deep to put into words.

When the kiss ended, he stood. "Let's get busy filling the bread machines for the morning's baking. You look beat, and I'm taking you straight home to your bed."

She rose and, in spite of a long day, she felt as if she could pirouette around the room with joy. *Thank You, Lord, for this wonderful man. Bless our love and hold back the evil that surrounds us.* She didn't know why she'd added the final phrase. The fires had ended over a month ago. Everything would settle down now. *Please, Lord.*

Chapter 12

The next morning, Audra unlocked the back door of her Victorian and switched on the bright kitchen lights. The yeasty scent of risen dough greeted her. Another day of baking sweet breads and brewing coffees. She blinked, still longing for the warm bed she'd left. She shuffled over to the hooks and took down a fresh apron. Her hands were healed, but Chad still worked the morning bake with her. She'd hoped to find him here, waiting for her. But no.

Then anxiety nipped her again. Why couldn't anything just go smoothly this summer? Tonight was the county board meeting. And on top of that she had a new, or really a recurring, problem. *Where are you, Chad? And should I call Shirley or Carter?*

Earlier, on her way down the stairs from her bedroom, she'd knocked on Chad's door as usual. When she didn't get a reply, she knocked again. Thinking he might have overslept, she'd cautiously opened the door. Chad's bed was empty. And no one was in the second-story bathroom or in Shirley's peaceful kitchen. Had Chad run away again? But why? Except for the nasty scene last night her uncle created, he had settled down and steered well clear of trouble all of July.

Now Audra paused by her phone. It was only a little after four o'clock, a terrible time to wake Shirley, who worked normal hours. She looked around her spotless kitchen and muttered, "Chad, where are you? You know I need you."

Then in the distance, the fire siren, summoning the volunteer firefighters to the firehouse for duty, sounded. Audra's breath caught in her throat. She raced out into the alley and looked around. She saw it then—smoke billowing farther down, a block from the wharf. She ran the length of the alley and out onto the cross street.

A sheriff's Jeep came up abreast of her. She glanced over to see if it was Carter. It was Trish Franklin, and she had Chad in the back seat behind the grill. Chad? Another muffled boom and Audra sprinted toward the fire. What if someone needed help?

She realized then that the storefront on fire was Hal's insurance agency. That stopped her cold. Images from Tom's fire flashed back into her mind with horrifying clarity. A scream tried to force its way up her throat. She pressed it down.

Not her uncle's office. No. It might trip him over the edge. Unable to stop herself, Audra began running again, though she was sure no one would be at the office this early. She was forced to stop well away from the fire. Heat barreled from the building. She stood there helplessly, watching flames devour the front of the neat, white-frame agency. Smoke billowed, mounting against the pewter predawn sky.

Finally, the blaring fire engine arrived. The crew in their bright yellow-striped outfits glimmered in the gloom. Trish came and stood beside her. Florence, Wilma, and other neighbors began streaming up the street, gathering around Audra and Trish. Wilma pulled out a cell phone and called Audra's uncle.

Audra wanted to shout, "No, don't call him!"

But of course, her uncle had to be notified. The thought of

being here when he arrived impacted her stomach like a balled fist. She wrapped one arm around her waist as if that would stop the aching inside her. She wanted to run away and hide. But she couldn't leave; the fire wouldn't release her.

The firefighters began to make progress. The smoke still billowed but water hissed as it extinguished the flames. The fire was nearly out.

She heard another siren, and Carter's Jeep raced up the street and rocked to a halt. Leaping out, he jogged toward Trish, looking very much as if he'd jumped out of bed and scrambled into his clothes. "What's up, Trish?"

Before she could answer, another car zoomed up. Uncle Hal's car. And then he was charging forward.

"My office!" he bellowed. "All my records! My new furniture!" He stamped his foot like an angry child and cursed.

The audience watched him with a combination of horrified interest, sympathy, and disapproval. Desperately hoping to defuse the situation, Audra took a few steps toward Hal.

—————

CARTER STOPPED AUDRA with a warning hand on her arm. He didn't want Audra in between Ramsdel and him.

Red-faced, Hal glanced over and then headed straight for Carter.

"Why is Chad in the deputy sheriff's Jeep?" Florence shrilled over all the noise.

All eyes along with Carter's turned to Florence and then to Trish's vehicle. That's all he needed—Florence pointing out Chad to Hal. Couldn't the woman ever keep her mouth shut?

"Caught in the act!" Hal boomed. "I told you it was that lousy, good-for-nothing Keski kid!"

Trying to ignore him, Carter turned to Trish. Another fire. Another failure. "Why do you have Chad in the car?"

Trish looked unhappy. "I found him about ten minutes ago just entering the alley from behind Mr. Ramsdel's agency."

"I told you!" Hal shouted, getting into Carter's face.

Some of Ramsdel's spit hit Carter's cheek. The urge to shove him away flamed through Carter. "Did Chad," Carter asked, gripping the slippery threads of self-restraint, "have any incendiary items on his person?"

"No, but"—Trish scowled—"he did smell of an inhalant. I thought he might have been using spray paint—"

"Well, you thought wrong!" Hal bawled. "I want that kid arrested and charged! He's a public menace."

Clenching his hands at his sides, Carter tried to step away.

Hal jabbed his forefinger into Carter's chest, stopping him. "Why anyone thought a lowlife like you should be sheriff, I'll never know! And keep away from my niece!" Hal added a vulgar description of what he declared was all Carter wanted from Audra. "That's all you wanted from my Sarah!"

Carter's self-control split wide-open. "Shut your mouth! Don't you dare talk about Audra that way. And don't blame me for your sins! Sarah wouldn't be dead today if you'd been a better father! Sarah was no innocent when I met her."

Hal threw a punch just as Audra leaped between them. "Stop!"

Hal's fist clipped the side of Audra's jaw.

Carter pushed her out of harm's way. She stumbled and fell.

There was an appalled silence. Ramsdel appeared to realize what he'd done. He shouted at Carter, "This is all your fault!" He charged back to his car and tore off, tires screeching.

Horror at the words he'd blurted out doused Carter's rage. Helping Audra up, he read disapproval and shock in her face. She turned away from him. Florence came forward and put her arms around her.

Head down, Carter turned away, hurried toward the fire

chief. He was angry with himself. How could he have forgotten himself and behaved this way in front of her, in front of God? The nasty truth about Sarah he'd held back for years had finally flown out of his mouth. Would Audra ever forgive him? Should she? Could he forgive himself?

— —

NEARLY TWO HOURS LATER, Carter sat behind his desk and eyed Chad, Shirley, and Tom sitting across from him. The three faces looked back at him—Chad defiant, Tom apprehensive, Shirley tearful. Would Chad have an explanation, a satisfactory one, for being at Ramsdel's this morning or not?

Carter didn't want to question Chad, but he had no choice. Why had Chad put himself right in Hal's path? Carter's conscience snapped at him, *Look who's talking.*

A spasm made Carter's right eyelid jump with nerves. "Okay, Chad," Carter started, "Deputy Franklin said she smelled the odor of an inhalant on your clothing, but no trace of your graffiti that we could see remained on the agency."

"'Cause it burned off!'"

"Where did you discard the cans?" Carter asked. Even his bones felt heavier, weighed down.

"I emptied a neon orange can. I wiped it in the bushes to get off the paint and then with my shirttail so there wouldn't be any fingerprints. Then I tossed it on the agency doorstep." Chad looked up truculently. "I'm smart enough not to keep the can on me after I'd done what I came to do."

"Tell me why you were at Ramsdel's this morning vandalizing instead of safely working at Audra's?"

"Why are you bothering to even question me? Everybody's got me charged and convicted already. I hate this lousy little town." Chad swore.

Chad reminded Carter so much of himself as a teen. *But have I come as far as I thought? Not today.*

Tom put a hand on Chad's shoulder. "Stop. Things are bad enough without you adding to it. Now answer Carter. He'll listen to you. He'll give you a fair hearing."

Maybe I have been unwilling to consider Chad as the guilty party. Carter's eyelid twitched again. *Maybe I want him to be innocent. But maybe he isn't.*

Chad pulled away from Tom's hand. He lowered his eyes. "I spray-painted the front of that jerk's office. That's all. I didn't start no fire, but no one's going to believe that, and you know it."

How could you be that stupid, Chad, after everything that's happened this summer? "Why did you spray-paint the agency?" Carter picked up a paper clip and squeezed it between his thumb and forefinger instead of aiming an accusing finger in Chad's face.

Chad bristled. "That jerk called me names last night when I was working with Audra." He looked up, rebellious again. "My dad told me, 'Never let anybody bad-mouth you. Never let them get away with it, or no one will ever respect you.'"

Carter tossed down the paper clip. *And, of course, you can see how successful your father's been at winning respect.*

"Hey, Sheriff, you stood up for yourself this morning when that jerk dissed you," Chad pointed out sullenly.

Carter felt his neck and then his face burn. *Lord, I'd give anything to take back the words, the anger.* But that wasn't how it worked. Words spoken could not be recalled.

"Don't imitate my bad example. I was out of line," Carter admitted in a harsh voice that scored his throat. He avoided looking at his stepfather. "Chad, don't you see that you've merely lived up to everyone's low expectations? And why? Because Ramsdel is rude and insensitive? Was that a good reason?"

Each word Carter said to Chad turned back to sting him.

Ramsdel had succeeded in getting to Carter, triggering him to revert to his former immature, unredeemed self.

As to Chad's account of what he'd been doing at Ramsdel's this morning, it could have happened just as he'd said. On the other hand, it could be a clever cover story. Carter closed his eyes, praying for wisdom. When he looked up, he saw the appeal in Shirley's eyes, heart-wrenching understanding in Tom's, and the tissue-paper-thin bravado in Chad's. Fortunately, stupidity was not a crime. "Chad, I'm releasing you into Shirley's custody while we investigate this fire. Shirley, you need to accompany Chad whenever he leaves the house."

"You're not charging me?" Chad gawked at him.

"No. I can connect you to the scene but not to the fire. As of yet. I'll spend the day sifting through the crime scene, and if I don't find anything to connect you to the fire, I'll charge you with vandalism."

"But hey, if the fire already burned up the graffiti and the can, there isn't any evidence that I did any vandalism."

Tom spoke up. "Let's get this straight right now, Chad. We won't let anyone get away with charging you for something you didn't do. But if you went to Mr. Ramsdel's business and spray-painted it, you have to pay for that wrongdoing. No matter what the provocation—a good man, a reasonable man doesn't strike back."

Tom's words scalded like acid, etching Carter's heart with regret. *Lord, forgive me. Why did I ever think I had the temperament to be the sheriff of this county in the first place? I didn't conduct myself in a professional manner this morning. I acted just like Ramsdel.* Worse of himself, Carter could not say.

Shirley rose, dabbing her eyes with a tissue. "Thank you, Carter." The three of them filed out and Carter sat down again.

He stared at his desk blotter and saw Audra's face there—shocked and disapproving. Carter closed his eyes, trying to blot out the image. But it persisted in his mind's eye. His mind returned to this morning's arson, the sixth arson this summer. *I'm no closer to solving these than before questioning Chad. What if—once more—there aren't any clues?*

The receptionist tapped on his door and opened it. "Sheriff, you have a visitor." She waved in a tall, handsome, dark-haired man. He was dressed in casual but expensive yachting clothing—light colored slacks, a dark polo shirt with the right logo on it, a red cotton sweater tied over his shoulders, an expensive gold watch on his wrist. He was also obviously nervous.

Carter stood and offered his hand. "What can I do for you, Mr....?"

"I'm Gordon Hamilton." Hamilton shook Carter's hand. "We spoke on the phone a few weeks ago."

Carter gave him a quizzical look.

"I'd called Audra's Place and you answered and told me not to call again." Hamilton's whole face turned fire-engine red.

"I see." Carter motioned the man to take a seat. He tried not to show his surprise—and his instant animosity. This was the man who hurt Audra and rejected Evie. He drew in air and let it out slowly. He wouldn't lose his temper again today.

Gordon sat down and shifted uneasily. "I finally decided to come and talk to you because you need to know that I'm not the one who started this calling war."

Carter stared at the man who wouldn't quite meet his eyes. "Calling war?"

"I've never bothered Audra and never intended to. But right after I stopped at her café earlier this summer, the phone calls started." Gordon straightened the crisp pleat down the front of his trouser leg. "I think I may have sparked the calls, but I want them to end." Finally, the man looked up, both uneasy and disgruntled.

"You want the calls to end?" Carter was trying to put this together, look at it from another perspective. "You think Audra is calling you?"

"Someone keeps calling and hanging up at all hours of the day and night. I assumed it was Audra because..." Hamilton fell silent and looked down at his shoes. "I did something petty. I took my bride to Audra's on our first day here and made a show of her."

Carter gripped the arms of his chair. *You total jerk.*

"It was petty and immature. But I was letting Audra know that I've got my life together now and I don't want her causing trouble."

Carter found that his lips had pulled back as if he was ready to snarl. He forced them to relax and asked the obvious next question, "Has Audra caused trouble before?"

"Well, no." Hamilton wiped his forehead with the heel of his palm as if he were perspiring. "But right before my wedding, my father counseled me to keep a low profile about my getting married. He's always been afraid that Audra would demand child support."

"You mean you've never paid child support?" Outrage roiled through Carter. He made himself count to twenty. Counting to ten wasn't enough. "You realize that Audra is entitled to child support according to the law?"

Hamilton shrugged. "I didn't mean to get Audra pregnant, and she should have listened to me and gone for an abortion. Maybe if she had, we'd still be together. I just wasn't ready to be Daddy, you know?"

"I know you're a man who has—by his own admission," Carter said with scalding sarcasm, "shirked all responsibility for his own actions and has neglected to support his daughter."

"I didn't come here for a lecture," Hamilton growled.

"Too bad. Your dad is right to be anxious. If it ever came out that, with your obvious means, you chose to be a deadbeat dad, that would cause you trouble. And I can tell you that Audra is not the one making the calls. It would be completely out of character for her to do something like that. But I will ask her about this, and maybe she'll have an idea who might be calling you."

"Fine." Hamilton got to his feet, a man ready to get out of an uncomfortable situation.

"I'll also try to convince her to take you to court and sue for child support." *And I'll enjoy doing so.*

Hamilton walked out and slammed the door behind him.

Carter made himself keep his seat. He would have cheerfully gone after Gordon Hamilton and pounded him into a bloody pulp. *God, help me. I feel like I'm on board a ship on Superior in November, tossed on one high dark wave after another. No chance to get my equilibrium back.* He covered his face with both hands. *Maybe I should just go to the county board meeting tonight and resign as sheriff. I'm doing a lousy job.* Then he recalled Audra's sitting beside him in church that Memorial Day weekend on Sunday morning with Evie between them. He wanted that future with them. He couldn't give up.

―――

IN THE EARLY AFTERNOON, Carter shuffled up the steps of Audra's Victorian. On the one hand, he could barely find the nerve to face her. On the other, he couldn't stay away to save himself. In any event, he had to tell her about Gordon's accusation. Carter rang the doorbell. He took off his sheriff's stiff-brimmed hat and rotated it in his hands. He heard footsteps.

Audra peered at Carter through the leaded glass panel in the front door. She unlocked the door and stepped back, wishing she'd known it was him. She was a mess. And after her uncle's public tantrum this morning, she felt vulnerable in Carter's presence. Why her uncle's outburst should cause her to cringe at facing Carter baffled her. But she couldn't seem to shake it. "Come in, Sheriff."

Sheriff, not Carter, he noted. And she wouldn't meet his eyes. Trying to rein in his attraction to her, he cleared his throat. And then cleared it again. "I'm sorry to bother you. Were you resting?"

"Yes, but I was about to get up and go home. I'm taking Evie to the beach this afternoon." Head bowed, she folded her arms. "What can I do for you?"

The formality of her question wrapped around his lungs. He strained to draw air. The urge to drop to his knees and beg her forgiveness slammed through him. Clutching the fragments of his shattered composure, he continued, "I need to talk to you about those phone calls."

Startled, she looked into his eyes. She hadn't expected this. "The phone calls? You mean..." Her voice faltered. Of all things, did he have to ask her about Gordon today? Hadn't her uncle embarrassed her enough? Now she had to discuss the father of her child with Carter?

He shifted uneasily in the doorway.

"I'm sorry." Audra pushed her untidy hair back from her face, trying to pull herself together. "Let's sit down in the parlor." She turned.

He followed her into the unfinished room and they both sat down on creaky lawn chairs.

"What about the phone calls?" She chose her words with care, her face warming with more humiliation.

Carter wished they could be talking about anything else. Well, practically anything else. He didn't want to discuss her uncle, either. He sat forward, resting his elbows on his knees. "I know who Gordon Hamilton is to Evie." He grimaced. "He came to see me today. Hamilton thinks you started harassing him first."

"What? Me? Harass him?" she gasped, looking up in disbelief. Learning that Gordon had come to Carter and revealed their former relationship was bad enough. But now this? "What did he say?"

"He says he's been getting hang-up phone calls since he came north with his..."

"His wife?" Audra arched her tired back and looked away, unable to face Carter.

Her profile captivated Carter anew. So regal, so tempting. "Yes, he thinks you started calling their number because he—in his own words—was 'petty and immature' when he flaunted his new bride in front of you at your café."

Petty and immature, that pretty much summed Gordon up. Audra felt her mouth twist into a travesty of a smile. "I'm surprised he admitted it."

"Do you have any idea who might be calling him?"

Carter's solid presence tempted Audra. She wished she could nestle into his arms, safe and cherished again. But somehow this morning's scene had separated them, shoved them far apart. Returning to his question, she shook her head slowly. "Very few people know that Gordon is Evie's father."

"Who knows?"

"Shirley, my mom, Uncle Hal." When she mentioned her uncle's name, her eyes shifted away from Carter, unable to face him. Would she ever live down all the public scenes her uncle had caused this summer?

"No one else? Not your sister? Or Brent?"

"Not that I know of." Audra shook her head. "Gordon and I dated when we were away at college. And Megan and Brent were so young when I got pregnant and left the family. Really, I don't see either of them calling Gordon." She pressed her hands together as if in prayer and held them against her mouth.

"I see."

"I don't see any of them doing this," she repeated, pressing her hands more tightly against her mouth. *Except for my uncle. He might.* But she didn't want to bring up her uncle to Carter. "And why now? Evie's seven years old, and I don't care about Gordon's wife. I thought it was rude of Gordon to flash her around in front of me, but I wasn't surprised at his rudeness. He's jumped to the conclusion that I'm calling him out of what —his own guilty conscience? These calls might have nothing to do with me and Evie at all."

"You're right." Carter didn't know how she would react, but he couldn't stop himself from saying, "You should sue Hamilton for child support."

Never. "No. I don't want to have anything to do with him, or have him in my life in any way." She felt physically ill just thinking of any contact with Gordon. She shook her head decidedly.

Carter felt impelled to impress this point on her. He remembered how it had felt when, after his mother's death, his own father had turned him away from his door. His father, another of this world's Doyle Keskis, had said, "I don't have any time for a kid." He wanted to spare Evie that.

"I wonder if you're being fair to Evie." He hurried on. "She may never have any relationship with her father. But don't you think she might feel better if he at least contributed to her support? That would show that she had some impor-tance to him."

This had never entered her mind. She propped her chin on her closed hands. "I never thought of it that way." A sob for Evie coiled in her throat; she pressed it down. "I just didn't want him in my life after...I found out what kind of person he really was."

No doubt. Carter longed to take her into his arms and hold her, comfort her. He flexed his hands, working out the feeling.

Audra looked into his eyes then, so serious, so pained. She longed to smooth away the careworn creases in his forehead.

But would he welcome her touch? She was Hal's niece, and somehow she felt that his out of control behavior had peaked this morning and stained her somehow. Perhaps she carried the shame because her uncle didn't have the sense to feel shame? Her uncle was headed toward self-destruction, destroying everyone and every relationship in his path.

And he was trying to destroy the sheriff's career. To her eyes today, looking haggard, Carter didn't appear to be the same confident man who'd wooed her this summer. *Maybe I don't have good sense about men. Maybe if I'd steered clear of Carter, my uncle wouldn't have...* No. Her uncle's behavior wasn't her fault— even if it felt as if it stained her, too. Was there a way to turn this around?

She lowered her face into her hands and changed topics. "Have you made any progress in finding out who set today's fire?"

Carter frowned, not wanting to admit more failure. "Trish and I have been all over the fire scene."

"And?"

"And this time the arsonist probably connected a slow-acting fuse to several handmade pipe bombs."

"Inside the office?"

"Yes, there was an obvious point of entry. One of the windows had been forced."

When would this all end? She sighed, so tired. "No clues again?"

"Except for the remains of the blown-up pipe bombs, all we found was a handful of blackened pennies."

"How bad was the damage?"

"A total loss." The wreckage had sickened Carter. Even if Ramsdel was a jerk, no one deserved a loss like that. "Your uncle is going to have a hard time getting back into business any time soon." *If I'd solved these fires, this wouldn't have happened to him.* Guilt over his incompetence jabbed him.

Abashed, she moved her hands to each side of her face like blinders as if she could block out facing unpleasant reality. Would this fire finally push her uncle over the edge as she feared? "Why is all this happening? Why couldn't this just be a regular busy summer?"

He thought he heard tears in her voice. Everything in him wanted to reach out and pull her to him. But her eyes had warned him away. His lack of restraint ruined everything that morning. Destroyed everything.

Through the un-curtained bow window which faced the wharf, Carter glimpsed the WFJW-TV van drive past. Great. Just what he needed, another story on the "Penny Arsons." And it looked as though tonight's county board meeting might be taped for the news. He thought, with rich irony, it couldn't get much better than that.

Chapter 13

The county board meeting took place in Winfield's town hall, a simple white-frame building a block down from Audra's Place on a side street. Audra approached its double doors, open to let in the evening lake breeze. Determination stiffened her spine as she scanned the gathering for her uncle and for Carter. She wouldn't let Carter face her uncle alone.

It was quite a gathering. Almost every ancient wooden folding chair was already occupied. A few men already leaned against the back wall. But Carter was nowhere to be seen. Did he intend to stay away? Or had he only been delayed?

Her entrance launched a ripple of glances and mutterings. Well, of course. Everyone had come to see the show tonight. And the show unfortunately involved her relationship to Carter and Carter's conflict with her uncle. She tried to appear unconcerned and suppressed her natural inclination to shelter at the rear. She'd come to show support for Carter. So she strode down the narrow center aisle to the front where Shirley and Tom had saved a chair for her.

As she slid in beside Shirley, the county board chair called the meeting to order. The five wary-eyed board members, mostly middle-aged men in short sleeves at a long table, faced the audience. The chairman sat in the center position. Just two rows in front of her and dressed formally in a suit in spite of the summer warmth, her uncle fidgeted, jiggling the manila file folder on his lap.

Audra made herself sit very straight and gaze around into familiar faces. After this afternoon, she'd come to a decision. *I will not let my uncle's embarrassing behavior affect me tonight. No matter what he does, it has nothing to do with me.* At the first opportunity, she'd make that clear to Carter. She'd finally realized that earlier they'd both been deeply embarrassed, deeply wounded by her uncle's morning tantrum. That was what had caused this afternoon's excruciating politeness between them. But no more.

She was not going to let her uncle's self-destructiveness taint her and...her love. Also, she had finally realized that until her uncle had attacked her early this morning, Carter had not lost his temper. If Carter didn't note the significance of this fact, she would point it out to him. Firmly.

Now awaiting the coming showdown, she listened to the county board begin discussing the minutes of the last meeting. A few flies drifted in through the open door. They buzzed around, flying into faces, making people flap them away with their hands. People shifted in their seats and glanced over their shoulders toward the door. What were they waiting for? Then it struck Audra. They were all—just like her—waiting for Carter to arrive.

A few minutes, and there was a rustle of movement behind her and a surge of murmuring. Audra looked over her shoulder again. In uniform, Carter had entered and taken up a position, lounging against the doorjamb, observing the meeting. His stance seemed to say it all—he had come, but he was in command of himself and the situation.

A silent cheer ricocheted through Audra. Their eyes

connected. She beamed at him. He looked taken aback. But unable here and now to express more, she nodded encouragingly and then turned back to watch the meeting, her mood rising like a hot air balloon. She'd never been more sensitive to his nearness. No matter what her uncle said or did, she would be in Carter's arms later tonight.

Carter's presence infused the gathering with more pronounced restlessness. The board meeting droned on. The friction in the room heightened; it became a tangible force. It was as if everyone were whispering, "Come on. Come on."

Audra realized her hands had fisted in her lap, and she made herself relax them. No matter what was said or resulted from this meeting, she had nothing to be uneasy about tonight. Nothing.

At the rear someone else entered. Another stir swept the room. The board member who was speaking raised his voice. Who had arrived now? Audra glanced back and saw Brent sauntering down the aisle toward her. He slid onto the aisle seat beside her and muttered, "Hey, looks like I got here in time for the show." He glanced down at his watch.

Audra shook her head at him, disapproving his mocking manner.

Brent smirked.

Then the chairman asked if there was any new business. Uncle Hal leaped to his feet. "I have something I want to show the board."

Brent leaned close to her ear. "So the sheriff didn't charge Chad with torching my dad's place?"

Audra frowned and whispered, "If the sheriff had evidence that Chad set the fire, he would have charged him."

"Well, the fire-setter hasn't left much evidence behind, has he?" Brent sounded pleased and glanced at his watch.

Audra shook her head and turned her attention forward.

"I have here a petition signed by many of Winfield's citizens." Uncle Hal waved the document. "Many people here are not at all pleased with the performance of Carter Harding as sheriff."

A few rows behind Audra, Florence stood up. "Many people here saw the performance you put on this morning, Hal Ramsdel," she chided. Murmurs of support swelled on all sides. "What makes you think you can live here full-time for less than a year and tell us what to think or do?"

Her uncle swung around and stared at the older woman in surprise. "I have the floor," he blustered.

"You have the gall," Florence forged on, "to cause public scenes at the drop of a hat. I'm here to tell you that I'm sick of hearing you bellowing and bad-mouthing someone about something. I was there on the Fourth of July—"

Audra turned and gave Florence a big smile. *Way to go, Florence.*

Hal swung back to the board members. "Do I have the floor or don't I?"

The chairman nodded to Hal. "Florence, Mr. Ramsdel has the floor. Please sit down and wait your turn."

Florence humphed loudly and plumped back down, making her chair creak.

"Wow, I love that old woman." Brent leaned close to Audra's ear again. "Hey, where's Evie? I thought she'd be here."

"She's with Chad. He's watching her," Audra whispered back, her eyes on her uncle.

Hal waved the petition again. "We've had six fires in this town this summer—"

Brent ignored his father and asked, "Afterward, do you want me to come and help you load the bread machines for tomorrow morning?"

Brent's unexpected offer touched Audra. She squeezed his arm. "Thanks." From the corner of her eye, she saw Carter make his move. He left the doorway and headed down the center aisle toward Hal. Carter's expression was guarded, as usual. But his stride was filled with authority.

"—and our sheriff has made no arrests," her uncle droned on.

"Well?" Brent prompted. "Do you want me to help or not?"

"Thanks, but Chad's doing that right now."

Brent looked startled. "What?"

Carter reached the middle of the center aisle and halted.

Hal continued, "Chad Keski was caught in the act of leaving my place this morning, this morning when my office was torched—"

Brent grabbed her arm. "Chad's at the café?"

Audra said, "Yes," looking past Brent to Carter.

"With Evie?" Brent demanded.

"Of course." She made a hushing motion with her finger to her lips.

Brent twisted in his seat toward the aisle and scooted forward, preparing to leave.

Carter halted right beside him in the narrow aisle. He blocked Brent's exit. "You can save your effort, Ramsdel. I'm going to resign as soon as it's convenient for the county board."

Hal closed the space between them. "You don't fool me. You come here tonight all noble and say you're going to resign—"

Brent glanced at his watch and jumped up, trying to slip past the sheriff.

Hal reached out and grabbed Brent's arm. "But it's just an act! You think you'll get sympathy and look like the good guy. I'm not the only one who isn't—"

Brent tried to wrench free.

Hal held on. "You blackened my late daughter's reputation this morning—"

"I apologize for that. I was out of line." Carter's eyes sought Audra's.

She tried to tell him through their eye contact that she understood, that she didn't hold it against him. She nearly stood up as Carter's penitent expression drew her to him.

Brent struggled but his dad held tight.

Carter reached up and began unpinning his badge. "I'm not doing this for show. I'll resign tonight."

Suddenly a lot of people were on their feet and each one was trying to be heard.

With his shoulder, Brent rammed his father and then pulled free. He turned and collided with Carter. "Let me by!"

Carter gripped Brent by the shoulders. "What's wrong? Are you sick?"

"Let me go!" Brent yelled.

"What's wrong?" Carter demanded. "What's so important?"

Hal grabbed Brent again, trying to pull him from Carter's grip. "Leave my son alone!"

Carter released Brent. "What's the matter? Something's not right."

Brent tried to start down the aisle. Hal hung on to him.

"What's wrong with you, Brent?" Audra jumped up, fear suddenly expanding, pressing down on her lungs.

"Let me by!" Brent roared with frustration, fighting to free himself. "I've got to get to Audra's in time!"

"What?" Carter asked.

"I set a clock firebomb there!" Brent shouted wildly. "I didn't know Evie would be there! I didn't know anyone would be there! Let me go! The timer will go off in a little under ten minutes! Let me go!"

Total shocked silence.

"Evie!" Audra shrieked. She pushed past Brent. "Evie!"

And then Carter and Brent were plunging out the door.

Audra rushed after them. The town hall emptied behind them. They were all racing down the street and then to the alley. Voices shouting and footsteps hitting the pavement.

Breathless, heart racing, Audra ran right behind Brent and Carter. They charged through her Dutch door into the bright kitchen. Chad and Evie were at the far end. Brent shoved past him and dropped to his knees by the counter.

"Chad!" Carter ordered. "Get out! Now!"

Working at the counter in an apron, Chad froze.

Evie sat beside him on a high stool. "Sheriff, what's wrong—"

Carter and Audra lunged toward her child. Carter lifted Evie and thrust her into Audra's arms. "Get out, Audra!" He grabbed Chad's arm, yanking him, shoving him toward the door. "Out!"

Chad stumbled outside and halted beside Audra and Evie. "What's happening?"

Audra clutched Evie to her, barely able to breathe around the lump in her throat. *Dear Lord, help.* "Brent says he set a clock firebomb—"

"What!" Chad started back toward the door.

"Get back from the doorway!" Carter ordered. "Get back! Everyone back!"

Chad halted. Drawing him with her, Audra edged backward and sensed the crowd behind her move back toward safety. She kissed Evie's dark hair and hung on to Chad's sleeve.

⬚

CARTER DROPPED TO HIS knees beside Brent. "Can you disarm it in time?"

"Yeah, yeah." Brent was fumbling in his pocket and pulled

out a screwdriver. Leaning over, he cautiously slid something from beneath the counter where Chad had just been working.

Carter glanced up through the open door and saw Ramsdel standing next to Audra in the crowd across the alley. He looked ashen. Stunned.

Brent continued working, unwrapping what looked like cotton batting. "It's not very complex," he went on, but his voice quavered. "I have to be careful and disconnect the fuses from the clock. I just need to clip them in time."

Brent's words washed like ice water over Carter. Audra's own cousin had set a bomb at her business.

Carter thought that he should take over, send Brent outside, but the kid looked as if he knew what he was doing. And time was too short to take chances. And if he did the wrong thing, it would mean disaster.

"I thought everyone would be at the meeting," Brent sniveled, sounding as though he was nearly crying. "I didn't know Chad would be here or Evie. I didn't mean to hurt anybody. Not even Chad. You've got to believe me."

"Just concentrate on what you're doing," Carter urged, trying to sound calm. His hands became fists to keep him from interfering with the dismantling of the explosive device. *Come on. Come on.*

Brent was unwrapping a lot of duct tape from around what looked like a cheap clock and some kind of tubed fuse connected to three large pipe bombs. With the cotton batting and duct tape removed, the cheap clock ticked louder now.

Beside them was a handful of pennies. Everything clicked into place. This wasn't one lone act. Brent was the arsonist.

Moving carefully, Carter lifted his cell phone from his belt and punched a number in. "Dispatch, there may be a fire at Audra's Place. Can't explain. Just get the engines here." He snapped his phone shut. He sucked in air. Pressure tightened even his scalp. He tempered his voice again, trying not to spook the kid. "How're you doing, Brent?"

"Almost there," the kid muttered, sweat slipping down the side of his face. "Here it is."

Silence pressed in on them. Carter was aware of each shallow breath he was inhaling and then exhaling. And everything—every movement that Brent made, every color and every shape—appeared intensely clear to Carter.

Brent clipped one wire.

Carter stilled completely.

Then a second wire. Then Brent laid the mechanism gently down on the floor. "That's it. I defused it."

Drenched in a sudden cold sweat, Carter looked at the clock time. It had stopped ticking with less than a minute left. Carter shut his eyes, suddenly limp with relief. *Thank God.*

Brent folded in on himself and choked with sobs. "I didn't mean to hurt anyone. You've got to believe me! I'd never hurt Evie! I didn't know she was going to be here."

Carter pulled Brent to his feet and out the door. Time to read him his rights.

"Why, Brent?" Audra staggered forward.

Carter let go of Brent and hurried to her. He reached over and supported Audra, who was holding Evie.

"Why would you do this to me? You're my cousin. I've tried to be your friend, stand up for you." Horror colored Audra's every word. "Dear God, Evie was sitting right over it. She—Chad—could have been killed!"

Tears coursing down his cheeks, Brent surged forward, pointing to his dad. "It's his fault! He wouldn't let me go with Mom on Saturday! He said I couldn't quit working for you until the tourist season slowed down."

Carter was incredulous. "So you thought you'd put Audra out of commission and then you'd get to go to your mother?"

"And you set the other fires, didn't you?" Audra accused.

"I hate this creepy little town!" Brent exploded, white to the lips with fury. "I hate Chad. Every fire was supposed to get Chad in trouble. He lives with Shirley, and Shirley's good to him. I want to be with my mom! Not with him!" As Brent motioned toward his silent father, he inflected the final word so it sounded like a curse.

Carter couldn't stop himself from asking the question that had snagged him all summer. "And why the pennies?"

Brent visibly shook, tears still washing his face. "I left the pennies because I'm sick of his drivel—every time I asked for money, it was 'If wishes were horses then beggars would ride,' and 'A penny saved is a penny earned.' Garbage! We wouldn't be nearly broke and living here if he'd been better to my mother!"

Recalling his duty, Carter gripped Brent's shoulder and shook it. "Stop, Brent. You don't have a lawyer present. I have to warn you that you're speaking in front of witnesses." Sickened over Brent's naked malice, Carter began reciting him his Miranda rights.

Ignoring his rights, Brent went on as soon as Carter finished. "Ollie's was just for practice. I threw the Molotov cocktail at Shirley's back porch 'cause Chad had dissed me the night before at Audra's. And at Tom's place, I thought Chad would be the one who opened Tom's gate, not Tom. I thought Chad would be blamed for Aunt Lois's shed, and when he"—Brent glared at Hal again—"told me that I couldn't go to my mother, I pipe bombed his place. But he still wouldn't let me go. So I had to—"

Carter squeezed Brent's shoulder harder. "Stop."

This time Brent obeyed him.

"Come along. I have to take you in to be questioned and charged." Carter touched Audra's shoulder. "Please lock your door. It is a crime scene. Everyone"—he raised his voice—"show's over! You can go back to the meeting now!" Carter turned to Ramsdel, hating to look at the man, so shattered, his failings exposed to all. "You better come with me, too."

———

AUDRA FELT AS THOUGH she'd aged a decade this evening. Would the shock of watching Brent dismantle an explosive in her kitchen ever dim or fade from her mind and heart completely?

She paced the small area of worn avocado-green linoleum in the reception area of the County Sheriff's Department Office. The reception desk was empty because of the late hour. The 911 dispatcher sat behind a glass window to Audra's left. A half door blocked Audra from the hallway that led to the offices, the interrogation room, and two cells at the back. Audra glanced at the large white wall clock.

It was well after ten. Shirley had taken a tearful Evie home with her. *I should be home with her.* But she knew she'd never be able to sleep until she found out how bad things looked for Brent. And she had to make things right with Carter.

Down the hall, a door opened. Carter, Trish, Hal, and Brent stepped out of what must be the interrogation room. Trish led Brent, whose head was bowed, away toward the cell area. Audra swallowed a lump in her throat. Brent had a lot of nasty consequences to face. But he loved Evie. *Oh, Lord, this is hard, but help this work for his good.*

Carter and Hal faced one another in the silent hallway. Audra held her breath. *Please, Lord, no more fighting.*

"I still can't believe it."

The voice was her uncle's. She'd never heard him sound this way—broken, defeated, completely without swagger or bluster.

"It's been a rough night for us all," Carter said.

"What...will happen to my son?"

"He'll be formally charged, and he'll have to face the consequences of what he's done."

Uncle Hal covered his face with his hands. "This is all my fault, isn't it? And what you said this morning about Sarah was true, wasn't it?"

Dark filmy sadness draped over, around her. Audra pressed her hands together against her lips.

"I wish I could take back those harsh words," Carter replied. "But yes, Sarah's sins didn't start with me."

"I've made a mess out of my life, and my children have suffered for it," Hal admitted in a hollow voice.

Audra prayed silently for her uncle. *Open his eyes, Lord. He's broken and open to hearing the truth. Finally.*

"That's how it works. Unfortunately." Carter laid a hand on her uncle's shoulder. "The sins of the father harm the children. But a father can also make a real difference in a son's life. Tom made the difference in mine. My own father didn't know how to love. He died a bitter, lonely alcoholic. And because he'd rejected me, I was headed down the same path as Sarah and now Brent."

"What turned you around?" her uncle asked, looking up at Carter.

Feeling like an intruder yet unable to leave, Audra held her breath.

"I was seventeen and facing a judge who would decide whether to try me as a juvenile or an adult. I almost killed that kid, remember? I didn't expect Tom or anyone to come to face the judge with me. But Tom hired a lawyer and he was there in the courtroom. I was cold inside, trying hard to look like I didn't care. But I was terrified. Then I heard something. I'll never forget that sound. Tom was crying."

"Crying?"

Audra felt privileged to be a witness to Carter's loving words. She bowed her head and continued praying.

Carter nodded. "That's what got to me. I'd been disrespectful to him, broken every rule he'd tried to guide me with. And here he was weeping over me. I wasn't even his own son. And in that moment, his love broke through the hard shell around my heart. I turned around right then. It was his undeserved love that showed me the way God's love works."

"I've never had much time for God stuff," her uncle muttered.

I didn't either until Shirley showed me the way, Audra admitted.

Carter squeezed his shoulder. "God can forgive any wrong we've done and he can turn our tears into joy. He did that for me. He can do it for you."

The door behind Audra opened and her mother entered. "I just heard and I came right away," she said in a subdued voice. "Where's Brent? Is it all true?"

Audra turned and hurried into her mother's arms. "Oh, Mom, it's been awful."

Her mother hesitated and then she hugged Audra close. "I can barely believe it. Did Brent really try to blow up your kitchen with Evie there?"

Audra nodded against her. "Uncle Hal wouldn't let him quit Saturday and go with his mother early so he thought if he wrecked my kitchen, he'd be able to go to Illinois."

"Where is that brother of mine?" Lois's voice was suddenly charged with anger.

Audra drew back and lowered her voice. "Mom, go easy with him. He's really broken up—"

"Lois." It was her uncle's voice. "It's all my fault."

Audra turned and her uncle pushed through the half door. Then he and her mother were embracing.

"Oh, Hal," her mother said, her voice laced with sudden sympathy. "We'll get through this somehow. But you've got to stop fighting with Mary. You've got to think of Brent. He loves his mother."

"I know. You're right. I know." Uncle Hal choked up and hung his head. "Audra, I don't know if you can forgive me. I've made such a mess of everything. The things I've said to you—"

Audra ached with sympathy for her uncle, for Brent. "All is forgiven." Her throat was so clogged with feeling, she could barely murmur the words aloud.

"Does Brent have to stay here?" Lois asked, looking to Carter.

Standing behind Hal, Carter nodded solemnly. "He'll probably go before a judge tomorrow or the next day at the latest."

"Come on then, Hal," Lois coaxed. "You're going home with me. You shouldn't be alone."

Her uncle allowed Lois to shepherd him from the office.

Audra and Carter faced one another. Without hesitation, she closed the distance between them and put her arms around him. "Oh, Carter, what an awful day."

He paused and then folded his arms around her. "Audra, Audra," he murmured. Then he drew her down the hall and into his office. "I want to apologize—"

Audra stopped his words by pressing her hand against his warm lips. This was no time for coyness. "You have nothing to apologize to me for. This morning just made us doubt ourselves. But I'm sure now. I love you. And if you love me, nothing else matters."

Carter pulled her against him. "I love you. Always." His mouth dipped to hers.

She stood on tiptoe, wanting to be as close to him as was possible. She prolonged the kiss, letting her lips tell him how much he meant to her, how glad she was that he'd come into her life.

"God answered my prayer tonight," she confided, sighing.

"What prayer?"

"I asked Him to bless our love and protect us from the evil around us."

"A good prayer." He tucked her closer.

"The past is dead and can't touch us, and I'll never let you go," she murmured against his lips.

"Good. I'm not going to let you go."

"No more doubts."

"No more doubts," he agreed.

"God is good," she whispered.

"Amen."

AUDRA DIDN'T OPEN HER café the next morning. She stored the risen dough that Chad had measured into the dough machines in the refrigerator and would use it tomorrow. Later, she'd work the pizza trade, but she had a mission this morning, a mission more important than making money. Last night just before turning in at about one, she'd realized that Uncle Hal had faced his sins, Carter had faced his past. She needed to face her past, too.

So instead of brewing coffee near the bustling wharf, she hung a Closed sign on her front gate. Then she drove out to her mother's summer place. She walked into the silent house without ringing the bell. That was something she hadn't done since she'd moved to Shirley's. After Evie's birth, Audra had always felt disowned, like a guest in her mother's home, not a true member of the family. But no more.

Audra walked through the empty-feeling house and found her mother in a pale yellow lounging gown sitting on the deck overlooking the lake. Her mother put down the coffee cup on the glass-topped patio table. "Audra." Then she stood and opened her arms.

Audra embraced her mother and asked, "Can we talk?"

Her mother nodded. "Would you like coffee?"

"No." Audra sat down on the padded chair under the patio umbrella. She gripped her resolve and lifted her chin. "Mother, we've never talked, really talked since...I told you I was pregnant with Evie."

Her mother visibly tensed, cradling her mug with both hands. "You're right, of course."

"I want to talk now."

"You want to tell me off?" Her mother lifted one eyebrow.

Audra pursed her lips. "No, I just want, need to speak the truth in love. I needed you, Mother, and you failed me." Audra had to look away. A deep empty cavern had opened up in her heart. The barren place that was left when she'd lost her mother's love. Or thought she had. Audra drew in air and looked back up.

Tears had leaped into her mother's eyes. She wiped them with the back of her hand. "That's very true. But did it ever occur to you that I needed you, too? And you failed me?"

Audra cocked her head to one side as she tried to understand what her mother had just said. Fear like thunder just overhead vibrated through her. "I don't understand."

Her mother set down her mug and passed a hand over her forehead. "Audra, do you know how old your father was when he died?"

Audra pursed her lips. "He was forty-four. Why?"

"And I was forty-three. You're only in your twenties, so maybe you don't realize how young that is to become a widow."

Audra studied her mother's expression, her tone. *Lord, help me understand what my mother is saying. Don't let the wall grow higher.*

"I was devastated, Audra. I adored your father. We were always so close. I didn't know how I was going to go on without him. And Megan was only ten years old. I didn't know how I could raise her by myself. Without him. The lonely years stretched ahead of me..."

Audra pondered this, but wouldn't let her mother shift the focus. "I was heartbroken, too. So was Megan."

"I know, and that probably made you easy prey to a sleaze like Gordon Hamilton." She made a sound of disgust. "How can I make you understand? You came home for our first Christmas—without your father—and you told me you were pregnant. I couldn't face it. How could I handle being a widow, a single mother, a grandmother, and you having a baby without a husband? I was barely able to get up some mornings and face another day without your father. I couldn't handle one more thing."

Audra began to grasp her mother's motivation for asking her to give up Evie for adoption, but it still rankled to be classed as "one more thing." Couldn't her mother see how much that hurt? "So that means," Audra accused, "I shouldn't have expected your help?"

"Honey"—her mother leaned forward, reached for Audra's hand—"please don't take it like that. I'm not saying I was right. I'm only telling you why I did what I did. I should have found the strength to stand by you. I didn't, and I know I failed you."

Audra took her mother's hand, feeling tears wet her eyes. Finally she'd received an apology. But was it enough to fill the hole in her heart? "I needed you so much."

"I'm sorry, Audra. I can't go back and unsay the words I said. But when you went ahead and had Evie, I was happy. I really was. I admired you for taking responsibility."

"You didn't show it."

"By then I didn't know how to show you my true feelings. After the hurtful words we spoke to each other that Christmas"—she dipped her chin—"a gulf had opened between us. And afterward, when we were together, I always seemed to say the wrong things. I was always so uptight."

Honesty forced Audra to say, "I was, too. I know that I haven't tried to bridge the gap between us. It hurt too badly."

Her mother squeezed Audra's hand. "I decided that this summer I had to make an attempt."

Audra finally got to ask the question that had teased her since the morning her mom had invited Evie over for her first afternoon solo visit. "Why this summer?"

Her mother released her hand and took a sip of coffee as if flustered. "It's silly, really. Just one of those moments that pop up and hits us in the face unexpectedly. I was at lunch with my friends for my fiftieth birthday. We chatted, and then everyone was bringing out photographs of their grandchildren."

She smiled wryly. "And it suddenly slapped me in the face that I was fifty years old. I had a grandchild, and I didn't have one photo of Evie in my wallet. Then it also hit me that Evie was seven years old and I only had seven years left to get to know her before she started high school and didn't care anymore about getting to know me. And on top of that, Megan just finished her junior year in high school. She'll be leaving me next fall and..."

Audra half smiled in return. She felt the connection of a mother to a mother. "I get it, Mom. I get it. I already get chills thinking of Evie leaving home."

Her mother gave a half chuckle and beamed at her. A sudden, but very natural peace stretched between them.

Audra sighed. A gull swooped overhead, screeching. Out on the blue, blue lake, a parasailer was gliding over the gentle waves with a rainbow-striped sail. High above the water, an eagle circling dove toward the water. The peace of the setting washed through Audra along with understanding at last. Her mother wasn't perfect, but neither was Audra. She felt suddenly free, lighter.

Coming home that long-ago Christmas, she'd assumed, as all children did, that her mother was indestructible. And now she knew the truth—mothers were just women blessed with children. "Let's not be at odds anymore, okay?" Audra reached over and laid her hand on her mother's.

"Okay." Her mother rested her hand momentarily on both theirs. "Evie's a lovely little girl." She sat back and lifted her coffee mug again. "You've done a great job with her."

Audra tested the water of their new harmony and mentioned a name she never spoke to her mother. "Shirley helped me."

Her mother lifted the mug as if in salute. "And I'm going to thank her for that the very next time I see her."

The sliding glass door behind them opened. "Hey, Audra," Megan said, "what are you doing here? I was just about to drive into town."

Grinning, Audra glanced over her shoulder at her sister. "Audra's Place is closed today. Come over here and we'll tell you all about it."

Megan paused and propped a hand on her hip. "And will that explain why Uncle Hal is snoring away in our guest bedroom?"

Audra chuckled softly. Megan was one in a million.

"Megan, pour yourself some coffee," their mother instructed, "and some for your sister, and bring out the croissants on the counter. The three of us are going to have a long chat about many things."

Megan gave Audra a quizzical look and then stepped back inside.

"It's going to be a good day," their mother said, staring out over the vast sparkling blue lake.

"Yes." A very good day.

"I hope"—her mother slanted a look at Audra—"you're serious about that handsome sheriff."

"I am." Happiness bubbled up, frothy and sweet, inside Audra.

"Good. Evie adores him, and your father would have loved him as a son-in-law."

Megan stepped outside with a tray in her hands. "Cool. Does that mean I'm going to be a bridesmaid soon?"

Audra chuckled and then she laughed. Life was good.

⸻

"HEY, SHERIFF, WOULD you be here to romance my boss?" Chad teased Carter outside Audra's Dutch door that evening after closing.

Carter paused in the deep purple twilight. "Don't be so smart," he said, grinning. Though he was fatigued from loss of sleep, nothing could have kept him away from Audra tonight. She had told him she loved him. The memory still made him glow so warm and bright that he thought it might be visible to the naked eye.

Besides, another mystery had been solved and Audra needed to be told.

Chad's expression changed. "How's it going with Brent?"

"He's in a lot of trouble. But his father has hired a good lawyer and Brent's still a minor."

"I didn't know...I didn't know till this summer that Brent had such a jerk for a father. Brent strutted into our school last fall like we should all fall down and kiss his big toe, you know what I mean?"

"I have a good idea."

"I feel bad like..." Chad's voice faded away. "Like I—"

"Brent's setting the fires isn't your fault. But it pays to remember that no one has a perfect life. And the people that bug everyone most are usually the most miserable themselves."

"Really?" Chad eyed him.

"Really."

"Okay. Gotta go. Shirley wants me home on time. All this stuff with Brent kind of spooked her or something. She's been kinda sad all day."

"Shirley has a tender heart," Carter agreed.

With a wave Chad mounted his bike and peddled down the alley.

Carter approached the open door. Memories of going through the legal procedures of an arrest here for Brent played through his mind. But after Ramsdel had left with Lois, Audra's beautiful words of love to him had overwhelmed and broken through all the sadness of this day.

Audra stood in the doorway, waiting for him. "I knew you'd come." She opened the bottom half of the door and drew him inside. Then she shut both halves of the door behind him.

Though all he wanted was to take her into his arms, he had something else to tell her first. The solution to the final mystery of this bedeviled summer. "Brent was the one calling and hanging up on Gordon Hamilton."

She stared up at him. "Brent?"

"Yes. In May he told your uncle about seeing Gordon with his new wife at your café. Hal unfortunately told him of the connection between Evie and Gordon. When your uncle added that Gordon was not contributing to Evie's support, Brent was even angrier. The calls were Brent's way of paying Gordon back for you and Evie."

She sighed and shook her head. "Well, perhaps Brent did some good. A lawyer called me this afternoon and said that Gordon would begin paying me child support plus back child support next month."

"You're kidding?" Mixed emotions over this development unsettled him.

"No, I was shocked. I gleaned from the lawyer's careful phrases that Gordon's family was afraid a scandal might come in the future if people found out that he hadn't supported his birth daughter."

Carter felt his brows draw together. "So Gordon didn't grow a conscience. He just decided to protect himself. Wonder if his wife knows anything about this?"

"I couldn't say. But I know I won't be calling her anytime soon. Poor woman. She got stuck with Gordon."

Carter chuckled and then gave in and folded her into his arms. "It's all over."

"It's over, but we're just beginning, aren't we?" She lifted her face to his and smiled.

He kissed her, a sense of awe flowing through him. *This wonderful woman loves me.* His heart did silent somersaults inside. "I love you, Audra."

She pressed against him, breathing in his distinctive scent. "I love you."

The scent of garlic and oregano hung over them. He grinned, thinking that the scent would always remind him of this moment here with Audra. He framed her face with his hands. "This isn't the most romantic of settings for a proposal."

She grinned. "Oh, I don't know," she teased. "Remember the love scene in Evie's latest favorite DVD, *Lady and the Tramp?*"

He laughed out loud and hummed a bar of "Bella Notte." "You're wonderful," he said. He kissed her.

She wrapped her arms around his neck. "Take me to the beach, Carter. I want to walk along the shore with you."

Within minutes, they'd returned to their favorite spot on the coast of Lake Superior. Like a rippled ribbon of light, the beam from the half-moon glistened on the lake's surface, flowing right to them as if they and the moon were connected. "Sometimes it's almost too beautiful here, isn't it?" Audra whispered.

He clasped her in his arms. "I don't deserve someone as wonderful as you."

"I don't deserve someone as wonderful as you," she echoed. "Isn't it nice that God always has something better for us than we can even dream of?"

He stroked her hair and she leaned into him.

"I just hope," Carter said, his voice suddenly low and rasping, "that He can help me get a handle on my temper."

She stopped Carter's self-reproach with a kiss. "He will. And I didn't tell you, but I had a long talk with my mother, and our relationship will be different from now on. It felt good to 'speak the truth in love.'"

He inhaled her light floral fragrance and the scent of the pines on the breeze. "Yes. Please marry me."

"Of course. Now kiss me. Please," she whispered.

"My pleasure." He held her in his arms, feeling her warmth and knowing nothing except death would ever part them.

Epilogue

The day after Labor Day, sitting behind his desk in his office, Carter opened his mail. Outside his window, the highest maple leaves had turned bright red and the lower branches had leaves edged with the beginnings of gold. The apple festival was coming soon and life was good.

He and Audra were planning a winter wedding. Brent had been placed in his father's custody while the legal fallout from his fire-setting played out. And Audra had received her first check from Gordon. They'd agreed to put the money into an account for Evie's future education.

When he and Audra had told her little girl about their upcoming wedding, Evie had squealed she couldn't wait to call him "Daddy." Pleasure flushed afresh, warm and sweet, through Carter.

He opened another official-looking envelope. Gloom crashed into his world. Oh, no. He read the letter twice, its news bringing back the recollection of an awful tragedy that had hit Winfield seven years before. *If I'm upset and I was just the arresting officer, how will this hit Trish?*

At that moment, as if on cue, Trish tapped on his door and stuck her head in. "Have a moment?"

He took a deep breath and nodded. "Come in. I have a letter you need to read."

She looked puzzled but walked in.

"Sit down." He motioned toward the chair.

She sat.

He handed her the letter and watched shock and dismay take over her face. When she'd finished reading it, she handed it back to him.

He waited for her to say something, but she didn't—just stared down at his desk top. And he knew that this news would rock her family. But he was powerless to change that. Autumn would be bitter this year.

⊏⊐

DEAR READER,

I hope you've enjoyed the first book in my NORTHERN SHORE INTRIGUE series. Did you notice that people in the northern Midwest call soft drinks pop? I suppose it's because a carbonated beverage pops? What do you think? What do you call it where you live?

On a more serious note, Audra and Carter both made mistakes in the past. We've all done things we wish we hadn't. That's being human. But how wonderful is God's forgiveness and grace. Every Easter season, I go back over what Jesus was willing to do for us—be rejected, humiliated, tortured, and killed. And all for me. And for you. As Charles Wesley wrote in his immortal hymn titled, "And Can It Be That I Should Gain?" in 1738, "Amazing love! How can it be, That Thou, my God, shouldst die for me?"

I loved writing a happy ending to Carter and Audra's long loneliness. And I was delighted to give Evie such a great daddy.

I hope you will enjoy the next books in the series:

Bitter Autumn, Book 2

Fatal Winter, Book 3

Beneath Northern Lights, A Holiday Story, Book 4

Uncertain Spring, Book 5

Ominous Midsummer, Book 6

Though each belongs to the series with connecting characters and setting, each book can be read in any order. Happy Northwoods Reading!—Lyn

CPSIA information can be obtained
at www.ICGtesting.com
Printed in the USA
LVHW091647011121
702138LV00006B/1043